Seed of Change
Neil Van Heukelem

This is a work of fiction. All characters and events portrayed in this book are fictitious, and any resemblance to real people or events is purely coincidental.

SEED OF CHANGE

All rights reserved, including the right to reproduce this book, or portions therof, in any form.

Published on-line at lulu.com

A product of the Brainstorm Central Authoring Cooperative
http://brainstormcentral.wikispaces.com

Map by Neil Van Heukelem
Cover Art by Neil Van Heukelem

ISBN: 978-0-615-27491-1

Library of Congress Control Number: 2009900810

Printed in the United States of America

*Dedicated to Miriam,
my loving and supportive wife,
and to David Holland
and my mother, Anne.*

Chapter 1

Astrid awoke and her heart immediately began racing. Today she was going to the Moon. She sprang out of bed into a small, cluttered apartment. After digging through a pile of papers and tablets she finally found what she was looking for: an article entitled, "Orbital Platform Elevators: Rapid Transit to the Moon."

As she plopped back down on the edge of her bed, Astrid began rereading the Popular Robotics article. When she first heard about the concept, it scared her; a platform in space in a geosynchronous orbit, strung with miles and miles of cable connected to a station on the ground. This cable not only provided power to the orbital station, but also a means of traversing from Earth's surface to the station in tram cars using only a fraction of the energy it takes to send a shuttle into orbit with traditional rocket boosters. She could imagine the panic of being that high off the ground, secured by a single cable.

The more she read about how the technology worked, the more she liked the idea of a rapid transit system to the moon. Each cable was made up of hundreds of smaller wrist-thick cables, all of which had specialized functions. The outermost layers of cables were braided in a spiraling pattern, to create the least resistance and the best grip for the rollers of the elevator car. The inner layer functions ranged from supplying power and lubricant to the elevator cars to housing nanomachine conduits. These microscopic robots continually circulated through the elevator cable like a mechanical artery, repairing and rebuilding as needed.

Of course, there were drawbacks. Because the stations on the ground were physically linked to the orbital platforms, there was only a certain window of time when any individual space elevator station was operable. Therefore, these installations were built all over the planet, mostly in highly concentrated population centers. They had been carefully plotted at intervals across the surface of the Earth to maintain continual connectivity to the Moon.

These space elevators were generally only used by average people, however, as more affluent travelers had the luxury of their choice of spacecraft. The government subsidized the platform elevators to encourage tourism as well as the relocation of workers to the Moon and beyond. Therefore, the orbital platform elevators were considered public transportation. Upon arriving on the orbital platform, ferry shuttles would complete the journey to the Moon's port-of-call.

As Astrid snapped out of her daydream, she realized that she only had a couple of minutes to get ready before her escort would be at her door. She took a quick shower, and then she rubbed her special botanic blend into her hair and brushed it straight. She put on a comfortable pair of pants and a ruffled blouse and rounded out her ensemble by donning her watch and a gold baguette pendant necklace.
Astrid was a tall woman of Scandinavian descent in her mid-thirties with shoulder-length blonde hair and a kind face. She wore wire-rimmed glasses as she could not bear the thought of having someone tinker with her eyes, even if they could get rid of her astigmatism.

After packing, Astrid went to the back of the apartment where her home lab was located. It was more of a greenhouse than a lab, with all kinds of plants stacked on every possible surface and various lights dangling and emitting their own unique spectrums. She browsed through the rows, picking at the last few specimens that had not yet produced seed. However, she got lucky with the *vituberous agraria*. It was a thick and hearty plant with a wide stalk that narrowed into a head which bloomed with long, black, spiky pods. She squeezed the tips of these pods and managed to extract a few pale yet viable seeds which she put into a new container.

She now had over forty samples laid out in a carry-on case from her home lab. All of these plants had been chosen as ideal candidates for adaptation to Martian soil. She snapped the case shut and carried it gingerly to the pile of luggage by the front door. She was only supposed to go to the Moon to debrief the botanist in charge of the Martian Expansion Effort but she couldn't help wondering how amazing it would be to see Mars.

There was a knock at the door. Leaning over her pile of equipment and personal effects, she waved the lock and the door slid open. In the hallway were two skinny men, standing side by side. They looked nearly identical with the same grey smock of Transgenix lab assistants and neatly cropped brown hair. The man on the left stepped forward, offering his hand and said, "Ms. Nielson, my name is Errol and this is Peter. We're your escort."

Astrid shook the men's hands, and began to bundle her things into the waiting helpers' arms. She flung her backpack over her shoulder and picked up the case of samples. Pete reached forward to offer to take the case from her, but she twisted away from him reflexively.

"I'm sorry; I would just rather carry this one myself." Astrid hurried, realizing the hurt look on the man's face. She carried her precious cargo to the cart, as Pete grabbed the last remaining luggage from the doorway. Pete and Astrid piled into the passenger seats of the Rascal, a small cart that was common in larger facilities.

"Looks like you got enough luggage to last a month," Errol chuckled, with his arm draped over the back of the driver's seat.

"I know it's only supposed to be a couple of days but I think I might extend my stay to take in the sights once we're done. I've never been off-world before," Astrid defended, as Errol drove down the halls.

They exited the dorm wing, and the cart made its way through a massive, domed atrium. This was one of many indoor gardens that were set up throughout the Transgenix Archology. They were not for research; these were just meant as oases in the otherwise sterile environment.

The Transgenix Archology was large for a lab co-op specializing in research, but they were the world's leading seed engineer and manufacturer. The archology itself was actually several large buildings that had been coalesced into a singular structure. This gave the facility a very patched-together look, with retaining walls jutting out at strange angles, and an eclectic mixture of architectural styles throughout the ages.

Transgenix gained their market share by developing a universal plotting system that maximized yields by taking advantage of soil and humidity variations. The company's role was to create specialized seed variations to increase the efficiency of this project.

This plotting system had exponentially increased the productivity of the world's farmlands by consolidating the needs and resources under a single governmental agency. The initiative, known as the Agricultural Resource Management, had increased the global government's popularity and solidified its mandate for a united Earth. It had also made Transgenix Laboratory Cooperative a force in the world market.

Now the company had started a new wing, as part of another collaborative effort with the government. This new division concentrated on engineering plant species for adaptation to other worlds. A whole new market would be available to them if this pilot project worked.

Astrid was lucky enough to be selected for this new group as she had repeatedly proven herself as an extremely capable and flexible scientist. The company seemed to value the latter characteristic more than anything else, but she was happy for the change. This journey would be the final step of this project, wrapping up a decade of research.

The group arrived in the new wing of the archology and Astrid's escort stopped the Rascal in front of the main lab and waited for her to collect the remaining samples that were to be transported. This was Astrid's real lab: a sprawling, 600 square meter open floor plan with a ceiling that angled steeply into a single skylight. The skylight itself was a brilliantly faceted prism that diffused the natural sunlight evenly across the entire room.

While it was a botanist's lab and all of the plants required the light, Astrid also found the natural sunlight very refreshing. Even the best solar-spectrum arrays were missing something you could only get from the real thing. After basking in the light for another moment or two, she went to the far end of the lab and opened a temperature-controlled safe where the remaining samples were being housed.

"Can one of you give me a hand with these?" shouted Astrid back across the lab.

In response, all she heard was inaudible raised voices from the hallway. She made her way back to the door and saw one of the lab assistants pinned against the floor by a man in the black and red uniform of a governmental Security Officer. The driver had also been pulled out of the Rascal and was surrounded by two other soldiers. She exited the lab with a bewildered look on her face. As the Security Officer spotted her, he released the lab assistant to turn and address Astrid.

"Ma'am," the Officer started with a brief bow toward her, "I'm sorry for the imposition but I have been tasked with providing you a military escort to your destination." He glanced back at the assistant who was just now rising to his feet.

"A military escort? Isn't that a little extreme? I mean, we're just transporting a bunch of seeds."

The Security Officer proffered a hand to her, gesturing back inside the lab. Astrid turned and walked back inside the lab with the Security Officer.

"Ma'am, I am Colonel Mazar, and I have been assigned personally to your case due to certain intelligence we have obtained indicating a possible intercept of this cargo."

"Just get to the point, Colonel Mazar. I have a shuttle to catch."

"We think there is going to be an attempt to steal your cargo during this trip. Your itinerary has been changed in order to provide a more secure route. You'll be lifting off with us in forty minutes from Tromso Spacebase," Colonel Mazar stated plainly. He pulled a letter from his pocket and handed Astrid the document.

Astrid recognized it immediately as Form 751ISC, Itinerary Schedule Change approved by her boss's superior, Allen M'basa. She reined in her skepticism at the sight of the paperwork.

"All right," Astrid said, reading over the document. "Let's get going then."

"That will be all gentleman." Mazar stared down the other TG employees. They looked at each other and then back at him in a way that seemed as if there was a mirror between the two of them. As Mazar took another step toward them with obvious intimidation in his gait, Astrid rose to their defense.

"I would prefer having them come along. It would make me feel much more comfortable with this whole thing."

The Colonel looked back and forth between the two assistants and Astrid several times before backing down physically and conceding the argument.

Colonel Mazar now drove the Rascal with everyone packed tightly onto the small vehicle. They drove out of the building and across the lot. From the outside, one could tell why the Transgenix Archology was nicknamed 'The Castle.' Many of the original structures protruded like minarets from the newer, domed roofs that ran between them, consolidating the building into one massive complex.

Transgenix used to be a few office buildings clustered together in downtown Tromso, but as the company expanded it bought the neighboring buildings. It had connected all of these buildings with skywalks on multiple levels and eventually the city of Tromso rezoned the whole area to the company and the building engrossed the streets.

The Colonel and his underlings had come in a much larger vehicle, parked in the plaza just outside of the lab entrance doors to the Transgenix Archology. It was a large, black truck that looked like an oversized van. The Colonel drove the Rascal right up into the back of the vehicle, into the bare, gun-metal grey interior. They all piled out and took seats in the rows of benches lining the walls on either side.

The military van took them south out of the city and soon the looming Ramp Assist of the spaceport rose in the distance. All of the most modern spaceports now had them; it looked like a giant, metal ski jump with a hangar at the foot. The ramp itself was contoured and long strips of solid metal ran across it like banding.

Astrid read an article a few months back in Popular Robotics about this technology. The ramp was a series of enormously powerful magnets that pulled a shuttle along and spits it out on a trajectory for space. This was another invention spawned from the movement to reduce energy usage for extraterrestrial travel.

The van pulled up just outside the hangar and they unloaded their cargo. The Colonel eyed the two lab assistants warily as they haphazardly carried the goods into the hangar along with the soldiers. Seeing the work that had consumed her for the better part of a decade carried past her in this way was unsettling to Astrid. In those cases was the culmination of nine years of intensive research and development, neatly packaged into four armloads.

Once inside the hangar, they could see that the shuttle had already been prepped, lights were flickering from the cockpit and a steady blinking emitted from the wingtip lights. The change in plans had taken Astrid off-guard and she was only now realized the enormity of it. No civilians were allowed into SecOps hangars like this, let alone allowed to be on board an extra-atmospheric shuttle like the one in front of them.

Looking at the shuttle, she could tell why the ramp was contoured as it was. The shuttle bulged to fill the contour perfectly, its cockpit protruding from the egg-shaped body in the front and the wings connected to the backbone of the craft on top. The only other distinguishing features on the hull were a cluster of long ailerons in the back.

Colonel Mazar led them aboard via an airlock door and upon entering, there was a well-appointed interior rich with colorful drapes and plush furniture. "It's an ambassadorial shuttle," Mazar defended as if the opulence were a negative. "Only thing we could get our hands on at such short notice."

"I think it will do quite nicely," Astrid replied, finally starting to feel at ease.

"We had better go strap in," Mazar replied getting back to business. "These take-offs are pretty rough for someone who's never been off-world." Taking her cues from her personal military escort, Astrid followed suit

They crossed what was apparently a parlor and into a split-level staircase that went up three flights, with narrow hallways leading off at every half-level. One of the privates led the climb, followed by Errol and Pete and then Astrid, with Mazar bringing up the rear. He led the troupe to the second highest level which led down a long hallway to a utility area. There was a vault on the far wall and what looked like lockers lining the hallway.

Mazar edged past the group to the safe door which he promptly unlocked, jealously guarding the keypad as he entered the code. The four cases were stacked one on top of another, just barely fitting into the allotted space. Mazar closed and locked the door and turned to brush past the group.

He led them up the remaining half-flight to a long gallery just behind the cockpit of the spacecraft. They each grabbed a seat and the two soldiers came around to check the three civilians' harnesses. Astrid felt giddy with excitement.

This is really it. I'm going off-world in a private shuttle. I wonder what my mother would say?

After everyone was belted in, a whining not from the ship but from the hangar grew in intensity, echoing around them. A few clunking metal-on-metal sounds chimed and a fuzzy voice came through over the cabin's intercom.

"Checklist complete. Take-off in...Five, Four, Three... "

Aren't we supposed to taxi or something?

"Two, One."

A hammer of force pummeled Astrid and pushed her deeper and deeper into the backrest of her chair. She could feel her brain pushing against the back of her skull, the G-forces pulling the blood from her head. She began to see spots on the outside of her vision. Feeling the faint coming on, she screamed.

Chapter 2

Astrid shrieked as the pressure inside her skull suffocated her brain. As quickly as it started, it was over. The G-forces lifted off of her body as the acceleration of the spacecraft dropped to zero. Suddenly quite nauseous, she turned her head and dry heaved a couple of times, realizing she had not eaten anything in the last twenty-four hours. Sitting back to regain control over her heaving diaphragm, she observed the sky though the portholes on either side of the passenger cabin. The sky faded from a dark blue to a solid black as they left Earth behind.

Colonel Mazar rose and came over to Astrid. "Here let me help you with those" he said, gesturing to the harness.

"Thank you," Astrid replied queasily.

"You know, I don't think I'll ever get used to these take-offs" Mazar offered. "It's a lot faster than taking a 'turtle' though," he finished as he popped her harness off. Turning away from Astrid's raised eyebrow, the Colonel gazed out of the nearest window.

The space elevator climbed gently into the sky on the port side of the craft. Its cable draped from the platform to ease the angle of ascent for the train of cars rising far below. They were painted green and yellow, and at the speed they were traveling it was no wonder how the cars became known as 'turtles'. Astrid found herself pressed against the window, taking in all she could about the miraculous system. At that thought, her mind turned to the vehicle in which she was now travelling.

Astrid turned around to face Colonel Mazar, who was standing at ease in the aisle facing her. All of the other passengers had left the passenger compartment.

"This ship is amazing! I remember reading an article about them once, though I must admit I didn't realize the take-offs would be so violent." Astrid paused to look around. "And it's so decadent!"

Astrid stood there taking in the opulence of this functional space. The seats were lavishly upholstered in a thick suede cloth and it felt as if there were three inches of padding under the carpet.

Mazar observed Astrid bouncing on her heels on the carpet. "Artificial gravity makes people feel a little off, but you get used to it fast."

Wide-eyed as a toddler exploring her environment for the first time, Astrid strolled out of the cabin feeling the extra springiness in her step.

"As for the ship, it's a standard mag-boost shuttle PC-111, aka Peacock," Mazar rambled, "it's just fancier on the inside because this particular craft is designated for high-value personnel transport."

"Well that was sweet of you to arrange," Astrid joked, giving the officer a half-turn and a smile.

Mazar returned the joke with an up-tick in the corner of his mouth and said, "Why don't you look around and I'll catch up to you."

She made her way down each passage on a self-guided tour of the ship. After passing the vault where the seeds had been stowed, Astrid came to the forward bulkheads. She found her personal effects in a bin in one of the small rooms, secured for the turbulent takeoff.

The next level down was the engine suite. There was a short hall that branched into three sealed doors. Turning around she made her way to the next half-level, a balcony over the parlor with the starboard and port bulkhead doors on either side. The last half-level was a hallway leading to what a sign over the lintel labeled "Mechanical." The bottom floor was the parlor through which she had entered earlier, decorated in deep reds and accents of gold.

Astrid flopped over the armrest on one of the plush, red couches in the sitting area. She felt like a weight had been lifted off her shoulders, and it wasn't just the sensation of artificial gravity. She suddenly felt unburdened. Astrid realized it was because the Colonel wasn't currently hovering over her. She hated it when people did that in the lab, she hated it when people did it anywhere.

Astrid enjoyed a couple of minutes in silence, her arm draped over her face, until she spied Errol descending the tall staircase with a sandwich in hand. Her stomach growling gave away the impression that she was sleeping, so she sat up.

"I don't think I remembered to eat today." Astrid said as Errol sat across from her.

Errol smiled and passed the meal to her. "This is pretty crazy, huh doctor," Errol remarked. "I sure didn't think I was ever going to be in a ship like this." He looked around at the luxurious accommodations surrounding them. Astrid began eating, oblivious to Errol's ramblings.

"Doctor, I know this isn't the best time, but I am such a huge fan of your research. I am an aspiring botanist, like you. Well, no, you're well established in your career. But I've read all of your published findings. Do you think you...?"

A clanging of boots on the last few steps of the staircase made Errol lose his train of thought and look up. Colonel Mazar was standing at the foot of the staircase with a black case in his hands. "Clear out boy. I need a word with Dr. Nielsen." Errol looked between the Doctor and the Colonel.

"A private word."

Errol stood reluctantly and left the room as Colonel Mazar shuffled Astrid to the far side of the room. "Listen, doctor. I need you to be careful. I already told you I have information that there's supposed to be an attempt on this cargo."

"Yeah, I thought that's why we took the private spacecraft."

"You miss the point," Mazar sighed, rubbing his forehead. "When I say there's going to be an attempt, I don't mean that someone is going to try to snatch the goods and make a quick getaway. The payoff of what you're carrying on the black market is unimaginable. When I say there's going to be an attempt, I mean more than likely we have a mole on board."

"Those guys? No, they work for Transgenix." Astrid said.

"Are you sure about that?"

Feeling patronized, Astrid started getting frustrated. "And that's why the samples are locked up in the safe. I think its overkill but it's not hurting anything."

"Yes, the samples are safe. But what about this?" Mazar said, holding up the black case he had been holding.

"Oh, is that mine?" Astrid retorted.

"I got it out of your luggage. I imagine it has all of the logs from all of the research we've had you do in the last decade." Mazar sneered inadvertently at these last words. He instantly regained his composure and continued. "And it was lying out where anyone can find it."

"Well here, pass it over to me. I'll put my brother's 'Magic Encryption' on it. He swears by this algorithm," Astrid said, suddenly brimming with confidence in her problem-solving ability.

As Astrid booted up the machine, she instantly recognized that something was wrong. The computer went right to the formatting display, as if the machine had never been used before. She turned the monitor so that Mazar could see and without warning, he sprang to his feet. He ripped a canister from the wall and hosed the computer with thick, white foam. A second later, the mound of lather heaved and a diffuse red light shone through the white and faded.

"Someone aboard this ship wants you dead." Mazar stated matter-of-factly.

"What just happened here?" Astrid exclaimed, pointing at the mound of dripping white goo on the coffee table.

"*What* just happened was someone swapped your computer for a bomb. I'm more interested in *whom*." Mazar's brows burrowed deep.

Astrid stared, slack-jawed. "Then shouldn't we be dead? What is that stuff?"

"It's a fire retardant," Mazar said turning the canister over in his hand. "But it's also designed to resist the vacuum of space so you can use it to patch holes in case of emergency. It sets very quick and hard."

"So, you had no idea that..."

A clanging on the stairs perked Mazar's ears and he was off running up the stairs, with only a brief turn of his head to acknowledge Astrid to follow behind.

*   *   *   *

Timon was pacing back and forth in front a dusty, but space-worthy craft. It was a small cargo ship, a SEA-Sparrow, much older than most of the ships still flying these days. The acronymic name stood for Short-range Extra-Atmospheric shuttle. This type of shuttle was not popular now that the space elevators made travel so cheap. Timon had overhauled the whole thing when he and his clan dug it out of a dune nearby. Judging by the damage to the ship, Timon thought it had crashed. But with a little creative welding, Timon managed to create a double-seal on the breach hull by injecting a pressurized gas into the space between the two seals to both cool the surface and detect any potential leaks.

These SEA-Sparrows were an early design, with the heat shield for atmospheric re-entry on its back like a turtle's shell. The nose of the hull was still a little misshapen but it would withstand the vacuum of space. Timon ran his hand over the smooth, black surface one last time and smiled at his handiwork.

The rest of the crew finally arrived. There were three men; the first was shorter and stockier with a wind-chapped face. He wore a tunic and several scarves wrapped around his chest and head. The second was a hug man who wore a robe with a hood that covered almost all of his face and stood behind the shorter man. The third was a man of average build and wore a robe and a loosely wrapped turban.

"What's going on, Keto?" Timon inquired to the first man.

"It's our contact. He should've checked in by now."

"We're still going right? I mean, we can't pass up this payday. Look around, we got nothing left."

"You're right," Keto responded looking at the courtyard they occupied. All of the buildings around them had been swallowed by the sand, piling higher and higher. There were only a half-dozen entrances to the thriving catacombs below that were still accessible. The clan needed the money and support this job would provide to continue the restoration effort.

This place was once a thriving city, with thousands of people living here, a waypoint in the ancient world. Now, all that was left were these few rooftops which Keto's clan had to defend fiercely from the oncoming desert. These rooftops were the only way they could enter into the city below, and more and more frequently the weight would crush the spaces deep in the sand to be lost forever.

They called it Pirate Town now. Their meager tribe managed to survive here by the traditions of their combined nomad heritage. The city had become a trading post for black market goods and a respite for the fugitives of the world.

One day, a man came and met with Keto. He called himself Mr. Black, and he wanted the services of someone untraceable. The Tuaregs, who had always lived beyond the reach of the government, had been the perfect candidate. Keto had smuggled goods on several occasions for this man, but this time, something was different.

Mr. Black offered to put them on retainer and in turn the Tuaregs would perform 'services as needed.' Mr. Black was just what they had needed when he had arrived. The Tuaregs had been struggling with drought and the encroaching desert, and he was able to provide self-contained modules that the Tuaregs were able to use to preserve their buried city from the crushing weight of the sand.

"You're right. We have to go."

Keto turned and clapped his friend on the shoulder, sending up a plume of dust.

"Do not fear. God will provide."

Chapter 3

Errol was moping around the forward bulkheads, tinkering with his own luggage. He had been ejected from the parlor by Colonel Mazar. He was mindlessly going through his things just to keep his hands busy, when he came across his satcom.

The company he worked for, Transgenix, had given it to him to keep tabs on Dr. Nielson. A senior-level manager named Mr. M'basa had personally handed it off to him to keep in contact during the journey. This was as good a time as any to check in and Mr. M'basa probably wanted to know what was going on. He tried dialing in to the main sat-feed but nothing happened. There was some kind of static preventing any kind of connection.

Great. Just great. This guy'll probably be breathing down my neck now about how I didn't keep him in 'the loop'

Errol gave up on the satcom in favor of venturing to the cockpit to see if the pilots might have something he could use to make a call. He started up the stairs, but as he rounded the first landing, he saw Pete. Pete turned from the vault, door ajar with the last case of seeds in his hands. The other cases were stacked high in one of the escape pods on the right.

"What are you doing?!" Errol approached Pete with a combination of fury and incomprehension.

Without saying a word, Pete ran towards the escape pod with the last case as Errol charged in to intercept him. Pete swung the case of seeds at Errol, who dodged the attack and lunged in to grab the case. Pete let go and swung his arm at full force, the blade of his hand chopping at Errol's throat. Errol grabbed his arm to fling the man past him. Pete sprung to his feet immediately lifting Errol off the deck, rising to slam him down on his back.

The ruckus of the two lab assistants wrestling around on the stairs brought the two guards, Keen and Harpo, down from the passenger cabin.

"What the fuck?! These assholes are trying to steal the seeds!" yelled Keen pointing his service pistol at the wriggling mass of grey lab smocks.

"Don't shoot at them! I think one of 'em is trying to stop the other!" ordered Harpo.

"Well, how do we know which one is which? I can't even tell 'em apart when they're just standing there!"

"You pry them apart by hand, of course," stated Colonel Mazar, from behind the two guardsmen.

"Yes sir,"

A quick elbow by one of the lab assistants to the other's face broke the wrestling men apart and sent one streaking for the escape pod. The two soldiers were already folding in on the melee as the break occurred. The quicker soldier, Harpo, swept Pete's legs out from him with his arm before he could stand and run. Keen took his momentum into a falling tackle on the downed perpetrator, but Pete rolled over and kicked him so hard in the face that he was knocked out cold.

Harpo was in a three-point stance after regaining his balance from the arm sweep. He began to stand but Pete had already wheeled on his back so that his feet were aimed at this soldiers head. Crack, crack, crack. Three well placed heel strikes to the man's face crumpled Harpo's body as if it was a puppet and the puppeteer had dropped the strings.

Pete began to scuttle backwards, heading for the escape pod but Colonel Mazar moved with surprising agility. He double-kicked off the wall to jump over his downed guardsmen and land between the traitor and his escape.

Pete bounced to his feet to try and fight past him, but it was immediately apparent he was completely outclassed by the officer. The first punch was deflected with a stiff chop to the nerve cluster above the elbow that sent a tingling sensation up Pete's strong arm. Pete continued to fling blows at Mazar, who easily deflected them. Mazar then proceeded to knock the air out of Pete's chest by inserting palm thrusts aimed at his diaphragm in between every couple of parries or strikes.

After a few of seconds of this, Pete fell to his knees gasping for breath. Towering over the beaten saboteur, Mazar demanded, "Who sent you."

Silence and panting was his only reply.

"Who sent you," Mazar repeated crouching down in front of the spy.

"No. Shh. Don't. Nevermind," Pete said raggedly, twitching back in forth. "Who. Sent. You," Mazar repeated, this time hoisting the man up by the collar so his legs were dangling off the ground.

"Don't make me," the spy's voice cracked, pleading.

"I'll ask you one more time and then I'll start asking *mean*."

All that could be heard was the muffled sound of a bubble popping and smoke started to waft from the traitor's mouth, his eyes glazed over in death. Mazar let the body drop to the floor, clearly disappointed.

Why anyone would willingly get a cortex bomb implanted in their brain was beyond Astrid's comprehension. She wouldn't even get the data sort that the company kept pressuring her to get, which was one of the least invasive forms of brain implant.

"Ugh, that's *horrible*." spat Errol from the ground, massaging his jaw where he had caught the elbow.

Astrid was in complete shock, standing on the stairs grasping the railing. Mazar stood over the corpse for a moment before he turned so that he was between Errol and the escape pod. "How do I know you're not with him, too?" Mazar began to interrogate.

"Wha..? He kicked the shit out of me in case you weren't watching," Errol said, indignant enough to withstand the aches and pains in order to stand and face his accuser.

"We'll see," Mazar retorted and grabbed Errol by the arm. As he began to escort the suspect up the stairs, Astrid became acutely aware of her proximity to the corpse and scampered after the Colonel.

Mazar led Errol up to the passenger cabin. He put Errol in the first row of seats and leaned into the cockpit. "You can lift the sat-feed scramble now." Mazar said to the pilot. He turned back into the cabin and dialed in to the access point. It was a large screen covering the middle section of the wall dividing the cockpit from the cabin. "Say your name," Mazar directed Errol.

A confounded look spread across Errol's face and his lip began twitching as if he wanted to ask a thousand questions and all of the words got stuck in his throat on their way out. He gathered himself enough to state, "Reginmund Errol Berthould!"

Astrid couldn't help it. She started laughing hysterically at this jumble of consonants.

A moment passed before Errol's employee profile popped up on the monitor. His statistics all seemed to be in order as a picture-in-picture window popped up on the screen with Allen M'basa's face.

"What's going on?" M'basa exclaimed. "What happening up there? Are my people all right?"

"One of *your people* tried to steal the cargo from right under my nose; that is 'what's going on.'" Mazar replied icily.

"Errol? No, he's been with the company for over sixteen years. He would never..."

"Not Errol. His partner, 'Pete'"

"Partner? There is no partner. Just Errol and Astrid. What are you talking about?" Mr. M'basa exclaimed, clearly confused.

All eyes were on Errol now, sitting in the front row of seats. "All I know is, I showed up for my briefing and he was there too. The coordinator told me it was a two man escort assignment."

M'basa was talking to someone off-camera. He turned back, "but the situation up there is normal, now?"

"Yes, we're on schedule and goods are intact."

"Let me talk to you privately a moment, Colonel."

Mazar stood and walked into the cockpit as the screen blinked out.

Astrid was wringing her hands about halfway back from Errol, who still sat in the front row. As Mazar exited the cockpit, she stood, clearly agitated, and came towards him as he marched down the aisle. He grabbed Astrid around the waist and pulled her with him as we walked and said "Walk with me, Dr. Nielsen."
Mazar guided Astrid back the other way as she began grilling him. "How did Pete, or whatever his name is, even get into the safe?"

"Yes, that unfortunate security lapse..." Mazar trailed off as he approached the scene of the encounter.

He searched the body of the fallen spy and finally found a tiny black button. "This," he said, standing, "is a microrecorder. He must have planted it on me when I first arrived at the lab. He plucked it off of me as I brushed past after locking the safe." Mazar posited, physically recreating the scene.

"Well, what was he even going to do when he ejected in that little thing?" Errol said, following them down the stairs. He pointed at the escape pod.

"He wouldn't get far," Mazar said, continuing to rummage through the pockets of the infiltrator. He dug up a communicator from the inside of the man's jacket. "Unless he had some way of calling for a pickup." Mazar stood and turned toward the escape pod. He began tinkering with the circuit below an exposed panel and turned back with a small, black chip, dangling from cut wires. "And without this, another ship could have picked him up and blended in with the traffic out there before we would even notice."

"You're not going to get any kind of a connection if the satfeed had a scramble lock on it," Errol supplied.

"Errant signals have a pesky way of giving away your advantage." Mazar continued his thorough inspection of the chaos in the hallway, the noise rousing the two unconscious guards.

They sat up groggily, both apparently undergoing many of the same aches. Mazar found all of the cases and samples within the cases to be accounted for, as well as Astrid's missing computer containing the research log. He turned and gave Astrid a knowing look and, satisfied nothing was missing, he turned to address the group. "All right, good to have you back with us gentlemen." Mazar nodded to the guards slowly rising. "Keen, you get all this stuff put back in the safe," Mazar said handing him the research log. "Harpo, you prep the escape pod. Set a delay on a beacon from this communicator," he said doling out Pete's device to the second soldier.

"We're going fishing," the Colonel concluded and headed back up to the cockpit.

*   *   *   *

Astrid and Errol sat in the passenger cabin and watched as the trap was sprung. The lure of the escape pod beckoned the marauders forward, at first indiscernible in a small cargo ship passing through the normal shipping lanes. The ship deviated from the commercial flight path to veer into open space lured by the call of their comrade's beacon.

The Colonel had called in reinforcements from a nearby space station. The sector station housed the standard detachment of Space Marines for regular policing duties. They arrived in a large jet bulging at the midsection. The commanding enforcement ship began blaring a million-watt strobe as the arrest began to unfold. The pirate vessel floated there as four marines disembarked from the enforcement craft. The marines' humanoid forms were amplified by the heavy, space-worthy battle armor they wore. They jetted over to the airlock of the pirate ship and boarded.

It was only then that the Colonel seemed to relax a little bit as he heaved a heavy sigh in the plush passenger seating. He checked his watch, Astrid noticed.

"I don't even know your name," Astrid whispered, seated next to Mazar.

"No one calls me by my first name." he replied gruffly.

"Will you tell me anyway?" Astrid responded.

"It's Eli."

Eli. You're an extraordinary man, Eli.

Chapter 4

Astrid was finally starting to calm down after the traumatic start to her journey. She had almost been blown up, seen a man's brain melt inside his skull and almost lost her life's work. She looked down at her hands, which had been trembling since the shock had worn off. She was just now starting to get control back.

"You're sure we're safe?" Astrid asked Colonel Mazar, who had kindly offered to sit with her until she had calmed down.

"Pretty sure, though I'll feel better when I hear back from the Marines," Mazar calmly responded.

"We should be arriving in approximately one hour. Make yourself comfortable, I need to take a call." He stood and left for the cockpit.

Astrid, finally regaining her lucidity, sidled over to the window seat in the passenger compartment to watch as the detail of the Moon grew larger and larger. The surface was spotted as far as she could see with facilities branching off of one another. In the middle was a large sprawling complex made up of thousands of domes and hallways.

In the very center was a massive dome with a cluster of holes in the center. Hovering above this central structure was a matrix of satellites, each emitting a bright red light. Looking back to the right of the scene toward Earth, Astrid noticed a long tube-like shuttle heading right into the path of the blinking satellites. As it approached, the satellites nearest began to drift toward it. These satellites helped guide the car into one of the loading docks on the massive dome.

"Wow," muttered Astrid under her breath.

"You said it. I feel like I'm in some kind of dream," Errol said.

Looking a couple rows back, Astrid realized that Errol had been looking at the same scene. Astrid wandered back to where Errol was sitting and sat down.
"I'm sorry for treating you so poorly earlier, Errol. It's just that this whole ordeal has been a lot for a buttoned-down scientist like me to take in." She sat half-evaluating the truth of her statement and half-waiting for a reply. Before she received one she continued, "And thank you for stopping that man."

Errol looked over at her and beamed at the compliment. "Like I was saying before we were interrupted, I've been watching your research closely ever since this project opened. I've been trying to transfer into the group but they keep telling me that they'll put me on the next rotation. Nine years later, here we are."

His bitter tone froze the conversation and both of their attentions drifted back to the port-side windows. As Moon City grew larger and larger, Astrid could make out finer details of the city. There were massive solar arrays on almost every surface that stuck out above the rocky surface on the Moon. The only parts that were not covered were great transparent domes. These domes were filled with plants; huge arboretums on the surface of the Moon.

As their shuttle crossed into a remote corner of the city, they descended toward the hangar to land.

"All right everyone. Grab everything. I do not know if we're going to have the same shuttle going back," Mazar announced, marching briskly out of the cockpit in a finely tailored black pinstripe suit.

Astrid and Errol exchanged a worried look after the officer passed, silently acknowledging the unsettling voice and image of Mazar's.

The group, consisting of Astrid, Errol, Mazar and his two troops, Keen and Harpo, marched out of the airlock completely encumbered with all of their luggage and the four cases of seeds. The hangar they entered was raw and industrial, with exposed piping all over the walls and ceilings. Everything was a dull grey color from the bare concrete, metal pipes, girders and door frames.

Astrid immediately began noticing how strange the people looked. Off to the right, a group of four girls exited, all with wild patchworks of long, colored hair. Each one had a different color outfit that matched the color of her vibrantly dyed coif. They went by Astrid and her entourage giggling and laughing behind their hands, poorly concealing their amusement with the stiff-necked corporate types.

"Damn Mooners" Mazar grumbled, "They get weirder every time I come back."

Mazar led the group through the Arrivals section until they got to what passed for cab service here. It was a little cart not even big enough to hold two of them. Mazar spoke with the cabbie for a minute. He pulled back his jacket just enough to show the man his badge. They loaded their cargo onto the cart and walked on beside it.

As they went, the passageway began to get wider as other corridors converged. There were many smaller, branching tunnels leading to restaurants and all kinds of shops. Down one of these side passages, Astrid noticed a vibrant green room. It was one of the arboretums she had seen earlier during their approach.

"Where are we heading anyway?" Astrid inquired.

"You two have been assigned your own private residence, of course," Mazar stated. Turning to Errol while continuing down the hall, he added "Your company seems to think highly of you, Errol. I will too."

Errol was taken aback until he realized this off-handed comment was supposed to be an apology for earlier when Colonel Mazar mistook him for a spy.

The group continued through the main atrium of the wing, through a swarming throng of hundreds of people, towards the restricted wing that housed the labs and high-clearance personnel.

This atrium was designed as a respite from the cold, grey halls of the rest of the city. The great glass dome stared out into space as starlight streaked the room with a cool vibrant shade of blue. Several murals filled with block letters and swirling stylized figures covered the bottom of the great dome. On one side there was rudimentary scaffolding where artists were painting a second level of murals.

The restricted wing beyond the security guards was nicely appointed, with soothing beige walls and wall sconces emitting a soft, warm glow. The cabbie wasn't allowed past this point, so Astrid and the group picked up their luggage and cases again. Mazar silently took them to a room down a side passage and opened the door with a wave of his hand.

Inside was an octagonal sitting room with three doors branching off to bedrooms. The common area was painted a deep green and it was surprisingly luxurious considering how far from Earth they were. There was an overstuffed tan couch, a maple coffee table, and an industrial-looking desk and chair. Astrid had not expected such extravagant lodgings so far from home.

Exploring the suite, Astrid heaved her luggage onto the bed in the room on the right. The bed was inviting, with fluffy blankets and satin-covered pillows. Reemerging from her new bedroom, she saw Mazar and the two soldiers still standing in the hall, talking quietly.

Mazar addressed Astrid as she entered the green room. "I'll be back to check in on you in the morning. Here's the itinerary." He leaned around the door-jamb to type in a few commands on a screen on the wall. The screen flashed through several menus and codes to pull up an Earth-week calendar, with Thursday highlighted in red.

"That," Mazar said, pointing to the highlighted box, "is your presentation on your findings."

Today is Monday. So much for that nap.

"Just a few tips for you before I go. Everyone does their part to conserve water so don't leave the tap running. If you need to get away and smell the flowers, just pull up this map," Mazar tapped the wall screen again and a layout of the restricted wing popped up. "And find the nearest arboretum. Right here." Mazar poked at a closer arboretum than the one they passed on the way in.

"Well then, I bid you good night. Gentlemen," Astrid added, nodding to the soldiers in tow.

Mazar spun on his heel and marched away as his troops struggled under the weight of their cases.

Astrid waved the door closed and turned to Errol. "Oh my god, I can't believe they only gave me three days to prepare for this lecture. That isn't nearly enough time!"

"Don't worry." Errol offered. "I'll help. I'm your personal assistant. I'll help you put your lecture together. I know your research well enough. Like I said before, you and your work are such an inspiration to me; I think I've probably read every word you've ever written."

"Wow. That will definitely help, but we need to get to work on this right away." Astrid began to regain her confidence.

The two scientists powered up the holovid workstation on the desk. The small square box began to hum as it started to work. A ring of lights in a circle on the top began to dance around in a warm-up pattern, and then produced a hovering, three-dimensional image of a snake wrapped around a globe. The snake slithered around the planet once and opened its mouth as if about to swallow prey and a floating screen widened out of the snake's mouth as the rest of the graphic receded.

Errol began typing away as Astrid sat with her personal computer next to the desktop system and began the transfer of her research onto the holographic projection system.

"It's going to be a long night," Astrid grumbled.

Chapter 5

Astrid sat at a bar unlike she had ever seen before. A giant hexagonal window in front of her opened out onto the vastness of space, deep and dark. The window on the opposite wall refracted the setting sun through the shallow room, spreading prism light across the ebony counter. It would hardly be noticed by space-dwellers, but to her Earth-bound eyes, it was beyond magnificence.

Astrid found herself daydreaming as she stared at her surroundings. She had been up all night the night before, and only got two hours of sleep last night. The presentation on the new stage in terra-forming was coming along nicely but she needed to escape for a while.

She took a sip and held the pungent liquid in her mouth before swallowing. The 15-year scotch she was sipping went down smoothly. As she drank, she began to reflect on her life and why it was she did what she did. After all, she had spent over a decade on this project for the company.

Yet, after meeting Colonel Mazar, the fact that the fruition of her work over the past eleven years would not be shared publicly became more evident than ever. Even if Transgenix wanted to publish the findings the government, who had sponsored the research, never would allow it. At least not until the Martian terra-forming was complete and Mars was opened to settlers. Consequently, all of the other glorious applications for the strains that she had nursed from gene splices would fall by the wayside.

When she signed on with Transgenix she had visions of helping people, here and now, to solve their food shortage problems. After all, that was the mission that brought

Transgenix the status it enjoyed today. Instead, she had been cloistered far away from anyone that needed help, locked in the intellectual tower of TG Archology.

Astrid was over forty and all of her youthful optimism seemed to have been sucked out; she performed her experiments purely by routine. Yet, the last week had awakened a new self-consciousness in her. She realized, for the first time in a really long time, that she was not happy.

"This isn't what I signed up for," muttered Astrid into her tumbler of scotch.

"Sparkling water, *shukran*," said a voice from behind her.

Astrid swiveled in her bar stool to see a shorter man wearing colorful robes peeking out from under a heavy, beige tunic. He leaned in to the next seat over as his beverage was filled and placed before him on the smooth, black bar. Shaking out his robes to settle around him, he gathered them up at his waist and sat on the high perch of the bar stool.

The man swiveled toward Astrid and proffered a hand. "My name is Keto. How do you do?"

Astrid, now very much aware of how intoxicated she was, wiped her face unconsciously before limply laying her hand in his.

"My dear, I do believe you have had entirely too much to drink!" said Keto with a jovial boom in his voice and his red cheeks bouncing. "Come, come, let me take you back to your residence."

As Keto grasped Astrid under her right arm to help her up, a large shadow emerged from the corner of the bar and obscured the light from both of them. The large man, standing in the path of the sun through the far windows was dressed in the red-on-black Security uniform.

Astrid squinted, and realized it was one of Mazar's bunch, Private Keen.

"Gawd, can't I get a moment's peace from you..." Astrid drawled.

"I'm here to ensure your safety, Ma'am." Private Keen responded brusquely.

"Go away; I'm having a drink with my new friend, Cheeto"

Keto took this as his cue to sit back down in his bar stool and turn back to the bar, and Astrid did too. The shadow loomed for a few seconds more before settling back into the same spot it had emerged from.

"I'm not ready to go back yet. Tell me about yourself, Cheeto." Astrid said.

"I meant no offense, ma'am, and it's Keto. I would love to tell you all about myself," the jocular man stated, as he puffed up his chest. He took a long, deep breath and began. "My story is a unique one and a tale you might find very interesting. I was born into one of the last free tribes on Earth, the Tuareg. My parents were both born and raised in our tribe. As is law among our people, the family with the deepest Toureg bloodlines will lead the tribe. This duty fell to me."

Keto trailed off, looking glassily out of the window. His seemingly pasted-on grin sagged briefly.

Astrid mustered after a moment. "There are thousands of 'free tribes' all over the world."

"No, they are all registered with the government, just another extension of the net that has been thrown over us all," Keto replied sullenly. "But we Tuaregs are truly free. We live unencumbered by those who wish to claim our land or our lives. It's not easy, but the traditions of our people will live on, passed down from generation to generation, and unspoiled by assimilation."

"I guess I never thought about it like that." Astrid gazed off into the blackness through the glass and contemplated this unique point of view, that even the simplest associations can change the nature of people. "But where? I mean you talk about land but the entire world has been claimed by one region or another."

"That is one of our most cherished secrets, I'm afraid."

Astrid could feel the gears turning faster in her head. This man was interesting. And above all else, it had nothing to do with terra-forming and genetic florae alteration. She pushed aside the scotch and motioned to the bartender for water.

"I have to say, I am intrigued." Astrid stated.

*   *   *   *

Errol was intent on the holographic display hovering before him. Both Astrid and he had worked tirelessly day and night to compile the necessary data for an accurate prediction and create this presentation for the scientific community stationed here on the Moon. She had wandered off earlier today and Errol had not seen her since.

The presentation had simulations for all of the progress made so far, from the establishment of the first scientific outposts to the interconnection of the colony towns to form a global Martian network.

Their audience was to be a brain trust of scientists had been gathered from all over the world, geniuses in hundreds of different subjects, to implement the New World Orders mandate of a colonized Mars. This think-tank, commonly known as the Mars Expansion Effort, established the strategy for the terra-forming that was being applied to Mars.

The first teams of resident scientists stationed on Mars were forensic scientists of all kinds and astrophysicists. They had proved through material evidence that a massive meteor hundreds of millions of years ago had struck Mars on the side with forward rotation. This impact had significantly reduced the rotation of Mars, which at one time had rotated much faster than Earth.

Because of the composition of Mars and its lesser density and size, the impact had slowed the rotation so much that it had altered the internal dynamo of the planet. The previously molten core began to cool and the magnetosphere around the planet began to wane. The protection that the magnetosphere provided against the solar radiation was lost. The solar winds tore through the ionosphere and scoured the surface of the planet, cooking it over millions and millions of years with a constant bombardment of solar radiation.

So the question asked to the Mars Expansion Effort team was "how do we rebuild the magnetosphere?" The entire project was nearly cancelled due to the enormity of this question. The first step had been the most controversial. Theories of giant jet engines and subterranean fusion detonations were floated, but the rational argument was for vent drilling. After it was decided, the rest of the steps for terra-forming fell into place.

Vent drilling achieved two goals. First, there was no catastrophic event planned that could potentially wipe out all life in the solar system. And second, it gave extremely lucrative drilling rights to companies provided they would also work toward the greater objectives of the terra-forming operation. The terra-forming could be outsourced to corporations in turn for new resources and new territories.

The process of vent drilling consists of drilling massive vents down into the crust to vent the still viscous mantle as artificial volcanoes. The vents were impressive as the simulation graphic on the presentation showed. Each of the vents contains hundreds of vertical channels, peppered over a mile square. Lava occasionally percolates to the top of the vents, spilling over the mouth. All the while the dare-devil drill workers continue to drill new vents miles below the surface.

These vents, drilled all over the surface of the planet, create lateral force on the surface of the planet. By restarting tectonic activity that was known to have existed in the past on the surface of Mars, the viscosity of the plates will slowly liquefy the core of the planet and regenerate the magnetosphere that the planet had lost. The forced induction of the lava is one of the elements that create the viscosity to restart tectonic activity, but it also makes for a very dangerous job.

Based on the necessary plotting of the vent sites across the surface of the planet, companies had been given exclusive land-usage contracts in return for the operation and maintenance of the giant drilling. The initial ore exploration had left giant hollows that were then sealed off and contained underground on the hostile planet. Corporation-owned cities were established inside the massive hollows underground. These corporate cities had been in operation for nearly a hundred years, and the seismic activity was picking up on pace.

These towns were constructed a safe distance away from the vent sites but close enough to be able to have easy access to them for routine operation and repair. At first there were only drill workers, but immigration grew these cities into metropolises in their own right, perfectly able of self-sustainment.

Heavy industry was established within these caverns for everything from smelting metals from the native mines, manufacturing and energy production. The technology these industries utilized was based on ancient, "Industrial Age" equipment for its easy construction and carbon dioxide emissions.

The carbon dioxide emissions served a purpose of their own. The next step was to construct an artificial atmosphere for the planet to establish a base atmosphere to protect the surface. The carbon dioxide emissions provided a layer of smog which acts as a barrier for the Sun's radiation. This artificial atmosphere will also trap other gases below in a contained ecosystem, which is necessary in converting the atmosphere into breathable air.

The atmosphere of the planet was still a work in progress as was the tectonic activity. The simulation continued, however, into the projections of the next phases of the terra-forming operation.

Once this containment has occurred, native ice would be melted into water and stored in massive, underground aquifers. The water will be disbursed through underground channels to hubs spread throughout the Martian terrain.

This is where Astrid, Errol and the Transgenix Laboratory Cooperative entered. Completely engineered plants customized to thrive in the naturally-occurring conditions on Mars will be planted using this network of water. The plants will then convert the hostile man-made atmosphere of carbon dioxide to breathable oxygen. The presentation gives all of the recommendations on how to proceed with the introduction of the genetically-customized plants onto the surface of Mars.

There were all kinds of statistical breakdowns of the different varieties of plants that had been created. For maximum coverage, plants of all different kinds were made to thrive in all of the various conditions found on Mars. The idea was the more coverage the faster the atmosphere exchange could be accomplished. Then there were all kinds of lists, of each of the eleven Martian cities and their satellite hubs, describing the plants needed for each city's specific conditions and the servicing infrastructure that was needed. Next, were monetary projections and various logistical data, and all sorts of charts and graphs.

The last part of the presentation was Errol's favorite. He enjoyed the intimate simulations of how the plants would adapt to the native soil and how they were projected to grow and evolve.

Errol was tired now, but the excitement for this project continued to energize him into action. He literally passed out at his desk last night but slept surprisingly well, despite the contortion his body had taken. He had been up for several hours today, but Astrid had sit not yet returned. Astrid was also pretty run down this morning, and had left to get some fresh air or its closest equivalent in the encapsulation of Moon City. As it was the day of the presentation, he had grabbed a quick bite out of a vending machine halfway down the main hallway and returned to the desk immediately.

The last piece of the presentation was a time-lapse simulation at a wide-angle planetary view as the Red Planet is converted to a second Earth. The animation displayed Mars and its grey, hazy atmosphere transform into a brownish-green, splotchy ball and then into a startling likeness of Earth's green and blues. He would never see the full fruition of this work, but he knew how important this work was for the future. Errol felt very strongly about this and he knew that he would be remembered as part of a team that created history.

Just then, Errol heard a kind of scratching noise at the bar. He turned to listen more attentively as the door slid open to reveal Astrid leaning on the door frame, hair disheveled and Private Keen standing behind her.

"Hey Errol," Astrid drawled as she stumbled over the doorframe. "I think I can make it from here, *sir*," Astrid bit out as she pivoted in the center of the room to face the soldier in the hall. Keen merely nodded and turned to leave while he waved the door closed.

"Gawd, they're everywhere. I thought this was going to be a vacation and instead I'm getting stalked by the military." Astrid wailed as she plopped down on the couch, slouching down onto her elbows. "I mean they got us cooped up in this little room, working us to death..." she trailed off.

She put a pillow over her face and lay there for a moment. Errol did not know what to make of it. By the Earth-standard clock they were still on, it was not even noon yet and Astrid was completely drunk. He rocked there in his chair, not knowing if he should be checking to make sure she was breathing or not.

"Ya know," Astrid began suddenly, flinging the pillow across the room. "I've had just about enough of these late night cram sessions. I have two PhD's; I do not need to be treated like this."

"You're just tired from the preparation of this speech to the brain trust. I think you'll feel much better after you take a nap. Don't forget about your big speech." Errol rose and lent Astrid a hand to rise and shuffle into the bedroom, where she instantly flopped over. "Don't worry," whispered Errol, "Everything is ready for tonight."

Errol pulled her slippers off as he exited the room and closed the door to ensure her tranquility. Just for kicks, he went back to the holographic display to tinker a little more.

*　　*　　*　　*

Astrid awoke with a hammer pounding on the inside of her skull. She opened her eyes briefly, only to squeeze them shut again as the light from the doorway shoots through her eyes like a laser. Groaning, she rocked back and forth on the bed to gain enough momentum to roll out of bed towards the water closet.

The room allocated as the 'bathroom' was little more than a 5 foot by 5 five closet. The door sealed and the room itself served as a shower stall. Astrid stumbled forward to grab onto the protruding sink and splash water on her face.

What time was it? Oh, shit, I'm supposed to give a LECTURE tonight!

A heavy note of panic ripped her out of her stupor.

"Hello?!" Astrid squeaked.

After a moment of two, Errol came around the corner.

"Well, you're awake finally! Did you manage to sleep it off?" Errol asked inquisitively, his nose scrunched up in a nervous tic awaiting the answer.

Astrid turned to Errol with big, red, puffy eyes slitted only enough to peek out and rasped, "Does it look like I slept it off?"

"No...no. I guess not." Errol stated, his shoulders dropping somewhat. "Well, what do you want to do?"

"I'm getting out of here. I'm so sick of this corporate bullshit. Science is supposed to be for the benefit for all and we're out here on some crazy far-fetched mission some old fogies concocted as a solution to our real problems back on Earth." Astrid grasped her temple in pain after this rant and she took a few ragged breaths. "I want to go where I can help people."

"Don't you think you're being rash? I mean is this a decision you want to make now? You seem really under the weather, and I think you might be projecting..."

"No, I don't think I'm being rash," Astrid cut him off. "And yes this is a decision I want to make now, while I can do real good in the world." Astrid let this hang in the air a moment with a pensive look on her face.

"I'm leaving right now."

Errol just ogled at her for a moment. His head tilted sideways, his brain worked hard to try and detect any drama or exaggeration in her voice. Finding it clean, he awoke to the implications of what she was saying.

"What do you mean now? You have a speech to give that is the culmination of your entire career!" Errol eyes wide, continued. "I mean this has just got to be nerves, you are nervous about the presentation." Satisfied with that answer, Errol seemed to ease a bit trying to think of a solution to the dilemma at hand.

"Its not nerves. I just don't care anymore." Astrid pushed past Errol and fled down the hall with no more than what she had on.

Chapter 6

Astrid shuffled down the hall, wearing only a kimono-style wraparound shirt, linen pants, and her fuzzy, green house slippers. She felt crazy and sick, maybe because she was running away from everything her life meant or maybe because she had too much to drink this morning. She couldn't tell which; all Astrid knew was that she wanted something else. She slowed to a fast walk as she exited the corridor into a central dome, heading straight across toward the far passage.

There was no going back. She had wasted her life up until this point. Well, maybe not wasted. She had learned a lot from her upper-crust educational background. But she knew that there was more to the world but had never really experienced what was out there. The last decade she had spent on perfecting an artificial genome for her plants now seemed totally irrelevant. Now that she knew that they would never be used on Earth, like she had always envisioned they might.

I mean, just off the top of my head I can think of a dozen applications for these plants.

The whole batch was designed to thrive in desert-like climates so what better climate to apply them to but a real desert? All of the plants that Astrid had designed were specially formulated to serve a function. The *profundus radix peniculus* was an invasive root that created a hearty root network that can sustain other plant life. The *calx epotus* use a fierce looking spiny plant. It could grow hundreds of root tendrils which seek out rocks to entwine and crush. The plant's trunk roots then absorb the rocky materials and convert them into organic matter. Astrid's favorite, the *vituperous agraria* was designed to introduce key nutrients into the soil, converting it to allow for a phased progression of plants leading to the eventual importation of Earth plants to the planet.

She shuffled along, thinking, through the massive throng of people churning around her. Astrid looked up into the breathtaking skylights interspersed throughout the dome and looked around at all of the people that lived this tenuous way, in a giant, steel bubble far away from their origins.

These people could be helped now.

The poor Tuaregs struggling to survive and retain their ancient heritage could be helped now, they didn't need to wait thousands of years to terraform new planets. Astrid headed across the entire sector to meet up with her new friend, Keto. She knew that he needed her help and that made Astrid feel good. It was a nice feeling, to be wanted, to be needed, not to be taken for granted. Walking down a few more exchange corridors ultimately led her to a darker corner of Moon City. The paint on the walls was peeling here, revealing the metal underneath. She was probably several miles from her dormitory now, and things were definitely different on this side of the city.

The ratio of strangely-dressed local compared to the conservatively dressed visitors was reversed. Here it seemed that everyone had a crazy style of all their own. A lady had her hair wrapped around her head in a twist looking like a dollop of whipped cream. She wore dark streaks of eyeliner ending near her ears and both of her cheeks are pierced.

Around a corner were a group of adolescent boys all wearing similar jackets, with big square patches loosely woven together with copper wire. They all had the same print stenciled on the back in red paint of a screaming monkey in profile. As Astrid approached, one of the boys stepped out in front of her.

"You don't look like you're from here, dearie" the boy said. He had rotten, yellow teeth and a straggly, mop of greasy, brown hair.

"I'm not." The boy stood there eyeing her up and down. "Excuse me; I'm on my way to meet someone," Astrid said as she tried to edge around the boy.

"Ooooh, 'excuse me'?! Hah ha this chicken's got manners, eh mates?" The greasy-haired boy jibed, turning to his crew. He was shorter than most of the others, but from the way they all laughed and jeered at his prompting, he appeared to be the leader of this little band.

Astrid tried to dodge him, the door to the loading bay that Keto had mentioned to meet at was just ahead, but the little greaseball stepped in her way again and wrapped his arm around her waist. Astrid jumped back and broke his grip at the unwanted contact as the little ruffians gathered around to block her progress.

"Get outta my way you punks!" Astrid yelled at them.

"Oi, that's more like it missy. We're no good rotten thugs we are and you gotta treat us like that," the leader shot back, further inciting his posse. By this point, the four boys other than the leader were yelling casual insults at her and jumping around, getting their nerve up.

"You creeps, who do you think you are?" shouted another unaffiliated passerby. "Leave that poor woman alone or I'll call the goon squads on you."

Astrid heard a loud, grating metallic sound as the leader lunged for her. He grabbed the necklace Astrid wore and as Astrid recoiled from the attack, the chain snapped with a quick tug. The greaseball then turned on his heel and he and his posse tore off right into the chest of a giant, dark skinned man wearing a black robe. The man grabbed the greaseball by his jacket and reached for the hand that held the necklace but he tossed it to one of his fellows.

The rage exploded across the man's face as he took the greaseball by the collar and practically bowled him into the mob of cronies. He leaped across the hallway in a few bounds to grab the boy from off the floor who ended up in possession of the necklace. The man picked the boy up only long enough to wrench the jewelry from the absolutely stunned boy's grasp. Then he simply dropped the boy on the floor. The gang of young boys picked themselves up and took off at a sprint in the opposite direction.

The giant with the small trinket now dangling from his hand, looks confused for a moment as if not sure what to do next. After a few long, awkward moments, he clumsily steps forward and offered the necklace back to Astrid. Astrid shakily took it from the man's grasp, being sure to stay far enough away to be able to escape if necessary. The giant man lets his hand fall to his side as he smiled an awkward smile.

Peering around him, Astrid noticed there was now a wide, bay door standing open from where this giant had emerged. A few strangely dressed men milled around the entrance. After a moment, one of them shifted to the side and Astrid recognized her new friend Keto.

"Keto!" she exclaimed.

The short, rounded man smiled broadly, and shuffled gently through the throng of people gathered there. As he marched forward, two men turned and followed in his wake. The four of them were quite a motley assortment between the giant, Keto and the exotic garb, the skinny man carrying a wrench and covered in dirt and a scholarly-looking middle aged man wearing a long tunic.

"Ah, my dear!" Keto stated happily. "I'm so glad you came. These are my companions. This is Faraz," pointing to the beast of a man who had saved her from the thugs. "And this is Timon and Khalil," beckoning to the remainder of the group. "Come, come the hall is no place for a proper greeting." And with that, he turned around and headed back through the bay door.

As they entered the loading dock, she spotted the only ship in the dock; an old, SEA-Sparrow model spacecraft bent all to hell. There was a crew of stationers with matching coveralls swarming around the ship. As soon as the man introduced as Timon noticed the attention the ship was receiving, he peeled off of the group to trot over to the investigators. The rest of them were escorted to an auxiliary room in the far corner. As they entered, Faraz held the door and stood on the outside as he closed it behind them.

Now the group was down to just Keto, Astrid and the fellow known as Khalil. "It is so good to see you again my dear," Keto began, "and it seems you possess your faculties much better now." He waved a hand indicating she should sit. The two overstuffed, red couches were comfortable and a low table sat in front of them with a perfectly polished teapot on a heating stand and a tall, glass sheeshah. Keto began to pour tea for the three of them and Astrid continued to take in her surroundings. The walls of this former-foreman's-office were draped in rich tapestries except for the wall with the window which looked out onto the exterior scaffolding of the loading dock and the barren surface of the Moon.

"My apologies for the hurried introductions earlier," Keto said as he passed cups of tea to Astrid, "but I thought you might not be encouraged to join us if you were not familiar with my clansmen. Keto smiled at Khalil as he passed the man his cup of tea. "This is Khalil, our resident biologist. Khalil, this is Astrid and she has the most incredible knowledge of agriculture I have ever encountered."

"It is an honor," Khalil said, raising his cup to salute her.

Keto leaned back with the cup of tea, under his nose, breathing deeply. The light, earthy smell drifted up to Astrid's nose as well. "Tea is a very sensitive thing." Keto began contemplatively. "As my people say, 'the first tea is bitter like life, the second strong like love and the last is sweet like death.'" Khalil nodded briefly before sipping his own cup, and Keto just sat back, deep in thought.

Astrid was content to sit back and listen as this little greeting ceremony played itself out. She had never been directly exposed to anything so exotic before.
Astrid took a cue from Keto who had kicked off his slippers, and did the same. The thick shag under her toes felt good as it tickled her delicate soles.

Next, Keto reached for the sheeshah, freshly packed with tobacco. "The sheeshah is also fickle," he said as he lit the crown of the giant, glass tower. "You light it," he paused to draw smoke from one of the hoses, "and it produces smoke." Keto puffed out a few smoke rings and continued, "but whether or not you choose to smoke it or not is the issue as it only lasts for a time before it is consumed." He beckoned to the glowing ember in the top, exuding smoke into the room. Astrid and Khalil took up their own hoses and smoked. Astrid drew in a smaller amount and savored the flavor of the mild tobacco.

Astrid felt compelled to speak. "First of all, I want to say what a great host you are and thank you again for your attentive ear last night. But we have a few kinks that still need to be worked out before we can go anywhere. First, there's the matter of my obligation to Transgenix, not to mention my place in the current contract with the government. Then there's this whole mess with spies and government agents that has me a little freaked out, I mean you could be a spy for all I know, after the same thing as that asshole that tried to blow me up. And on top of that, there's the issue of what the hell I'm doing and where we are going to end up after I flush my entire life and career down the toilet!" She ended this rant in a squealing pitch, thoroughly agitated.

"Well, I don't think you'd be here right now if you didn't trust me for one," Keto stated matter-of-factly as he put his tea cup back down on the coffee table. "And all of these concerns have been looked to already my dear. You said yourself that your colleague, what was his name Errol?, was more than qualified to take your place within the company and the project. Your role within this project is to be concluded after this week anyway, was it not dear?"

He stared directly into her eyes as he enumerated her concerns. His eyes were gleaming with intensity. After a moment's pause, he shifted briefly before concluding, "And as for your obligation to your company, only you can determine that."

"Well," Astrid said thinking hard about her situation, "I've been a free shareholder for almost four years now, and I never got their stupid data sort so they can't be worried about me running off with trade secrets. . . ." Astrid paused and then tapped a finger to her temple, "except for the ones that I keep in here. And they have no right to those. I suppose, if the current project continues they really have no recourse on me anyway, though I'll have to kiss a good chunk of change goodbye for the inconsiderate way. . . ." She trailed off looking around.

Perking up, Astrid said "I guess you're right! I'm a free woman!" She stood up and stretched her arms high and wide above her head, smiling fiendishly.

"With your expertise, we can make a real life for my tribe. I want you to know how invaluable your services are to us Tuareg," Keto said hesitantly, afraid that this newly realized freedom might take his good fortune away.

"Oh, don't be silly Keto." She flung her arms around him and whispered, "You are setting me free."

"Let's not get ahead of ourselves, my dear. There's still much to do, though I am truly thrilled that you are so excited to be joining us" He smiled sweetly at her. Sitting down again but perching on the edge of the couch now at full attention, Keto continued. "Let me clue you in as to what we've been up to. . . ."

*　　　*　　　*　　　*

Errol sat uncomfortably in the green room in his suit pants and a plain, white tee after having been interrupted in his preparations by all of the fuss around Astrid. He fidgeted nervously with the commlink lying on the coffee table. In the next moment, Colonel Mazar bursts through the hallway door to command the room.

"Where is she?"

Errol jumped to his feet as Mazar entered the room and replied, "She came in this morning dead drunk. I couldn't believe it! This is the biggest single event in her entire distinguished career. . . ."

"Which is probably why she was dead drunk," Mazar said, cutting Errol off.

"Well? Go on."

"She came in around one, Greenwich Mean Time, and I thought if I put her right to bed she could sleep it off before the presentation. But, she woke up in a panic and ran off down the hall before I could talk any sense into her." Errol looked down at his feet to avoid the intense embarrassment.

Mazar stared at him for a moment, but then, unexpectedly turned to one of his armsmen. "Private Keen. You let her get drunk?!"

The flustered Private Keen began to stammer. "You said just keep an eye on her; you didn't say anything about keeping her sober."

"It was implicit in the instruction I gave you," Mazar shot over his shoulder to Keen, returning to face Errol. "Well, did she tell you where she was going?"

"No. All she said was something about being able to do 'real good in the world' if she left when she did."

"Hmm," Mazar said sitting in the far chair and waving his two henchmen away to the hall. "That implies that she has some thing or some plan that is time-sensitive."

Mazar stood perfectly still for a while and then squared against Errol with a wild intensity in his eyes.

"I've been doing a little reading on you, son. You have an impressive resume."

"Uh, thanks."

"How would you like a promotion to Project Manager? I've talked to your employers and they agree that your skills are more than adequate to pick up where Dr. Nielsen has left off. And we feel that your combination of experiences would be much better suited for the exposure of your new job title."

"That's...that's great," Errol responded, completely shocked.

Mazar stood up and dug into his front pocket, pulling out a small, black device. While he twiddled the controls and stared at the screen, he pointed right at Errol without looking up and said, "You will get ready and take Astrid's place at the lecture tonight. I have to go." And with that, Mazar walked briskly out of the room, issuing muffled instructions to one of his henchmen.

"Another of his magic tricks, I suppose," Errol mumbled to himself as he buttoned his shirt and shrugged his jacket on. After a bit more grumbling to himself, Errol examined the final product in the mirror and smiled. "Buck up. You got just what you wanted - you're the lead on this!" He spun happily towards the door, scooping up the disk with the presentation on it and tucking it into his suit pocket.

As Errol strode out of the suite, he was greeted by the soldier Harpo. He was an older man with a set jaw and a painted-on smile meant to reassure.

"Ready?" Harpo inquired.

Errol nodded, suddenly feeling the nerves creeping up on him, and walked slightly behind his escort through a series of turns to a narrow hallway in the corner of a grand concourse.

"Backstage is that way," Harpo indicated, taking up a post at the mouth of the hallway.

Errol proceeded down alone to a single door which opened into a high-ceilinged sitting room with a workstation in one corner. There were windows along the top of all of the walls giving the impression that you were in the bottom of a well. A thin, conservatively dressed woman with round glasses paced anxiously and at Errol's entrance lit up with excitement and then faded.

"Hello, sir. My name is Cara and I am Dr. Nielsen's liaison. Are we to expect her soon?"

"Dr. Nielsen is not coming. I will be filling in for her for the lecture tonight," Errol replied, and at the skeptical look he received, he continued. "Of course, I am more than familiar with all of her work and findings in this endeavor."

"Of course you are," Cara replied hastily straightening out her expression forcefully, "I meant no disrespect. It's just that I have a profound admiration for Dr. Nielsen's work and was looking forward to meeting her."

"Mm."

"Well, let me get you set up and you will go on as scheduled, I suppose." Errol handed the disc across to Cara as she continued talking.

"We didn't want to make any changes to this evening's itinerary unless absolutely necessary." Looking down at her watch, Cara looked back up and said, "Let's see, you've got about twenty minutes until you go on."

"Oh. Okay." Errol tried to slow his breathing down.

Cara retreated through the far door, and Errol sat, rehearsing the prepared remarks one last time. This was much easier when done in tandem with another, extremely intelligent scientist. As he was finishing his mental run-through, Cara re-entered and held the door to usher Errol through. Errol stood and marched through the doorway into the bright lights of the stage.

*   *   *   *

Mazar marched down the hallway, with his guardsman Keen trailing behind him. Mazar continued to glance down at his little micro display in his palm. He had crossed practically the entire northern quadrant of Central Receiving, one of the largest sections of Moon City. This side of the city was less cared-for, with peeling paint and cracked and chipped floor tiles and wall panels. The hallways were narrower and the whole facility had a seedier, industrial feel to it.

Mazar stormed past a gang of hooligans who eyed him warily and circled wide around him. Then he turned down another series of labyrinthine passages to a wide, unmarked bay door. After looking around to make sure no one was watching or following them, he slid the door open and walked into the darkness.

Once the door clanged to a close and the latch fell into place, Mazar and Keen brushed through a black curtain into the loading dock. Mazar couldn't help but stand there for a moment, grinning broadly. In the dock were a dozen Space Marine battle armor rigs, arranged in a wide four by three rank.

The first row of four were already occupied, slowly and deliberately raising and lowering the arms and ailerons on the shoulders and back in a motor control test. The enhanced humanoid figures of the operational suits were intensely menacing. They stood nine feet tall and were broad at the shoulders. Huge, black rifles nearly as tall as the giants themselves were slung over the shoulders past a squat head with a series of sensors like arachnid eyes.

The other rigs were still empty, with their operators and a fleet of technicians tinkering with the servos from the multiple maintenance panels all over the suits. The rigs without an operator looked like dissected bodies, with the chest retracted to either side and a wide collar lifted above the head to reveal the pilot's station.
The arms on the suit nearest Mazar were steadily raised and lowered, as a series of clicking and popping noises emanated from the forearms in what Mazar knew to be a

weapons cycling test.

A Marine in a black flight-suit with captain's tabs came forward to greet Colonel Mazar. "Colonel," the captain said, snapping to attention and saluting formally.

"At ease, Captain. How are we doing?" Mazar replied.

"We'll be fully operational in about thirty minutes, Colonel. As you requested, three squads of four will be ready to be deployed."

"Very good, Captain. You have your orders, carry on."

"Yes, sir!"

Chapter 7

"And so you see, we stand on a razor's edge. It's up to you," the chief Keto stated. He sat back on the plush couch and weighed Astrid's reaction.

Astrid was nervously excited. It sounded like everything that she had always dreamed of doing. "I understand that there is some danger involved but I want to help. I've always just wanted to help. That's why I dedicated my life to understanding the genetics of plants. I thought I could make a difference to all of the people starving all over the world."

"You are a blessing from the heavens, my dear! Your words are music to my ears." Keto smiled reassuringly.

A knock at the door, and the thin man Timon poked his head into the room with a frantic expression. "Inbound call from Mr. Black!" He yelled a little too loudly at Keto. The raucous interruption into their peaceful sanctuary shocked everyone in the room.

"Excuse my friend, he is easily excitable," Keto mentioned to Astrid as he rose to pad out of the room. He grabbed the door and turned back. "Come on you two. This concerns you both as well."

Khalil rose after Astrid and they both followed Keto out of the parlor and into the wider docking bay. Timon was racing ahead of Keto toward the utilitarian stairway leading up to the control booth, a wide and narrow sealed room running the entire width of the loading bay, tucking into a corner of the ceiling.

They all followed the squirrelly Timon into the room and the airlock was sealed behind them, as it was the only door between the control booth and the open expanse of the bay. A row of half a dozen monitor stations ran down the near side of the room, overlooking the bay and the middle terminal blinked with a giant red exclamation point.

Keto saw the sign on the monitor and visibly calmed himself with a deep, deliberate exhalation. He then gestured to everyone to take seats on either side of the monitor in perfect silence as if the party holding on the other line could hear everything they were doing.

Finally, Keto settled himself into the console chair and flipped a switch. "What's taking so long?" blared a modulated voice. The screen was blank, but the outgoing video feed had blinked on. "I expected to be done with this shit three fucking days ago!" The crescendo of this sentence lent itself to ear-piercing feedback from the terminal.

"We have what you asked for. All you need to do is pick it up," said Keto with a calm reverence in his voice Astrid had never heard.

Silence answered from Mr. Black. "All right then." More silence. "Show me the parcel."

Keto beckoned to Astrid with a come-hither gesture. She clumsily bumped around the console chairs to lean on the back of Keto's chair. She gazed into the tiny console camera with a look of a combination of fear and bewilderment. More silence. Keto swiveled and flitted a wrist directly in front of Astrid's face and immediately she was dragged off to the left by treetrunk arms. Faraz put her down on the other side of the room and stood between her and Keto, smiling a benign smile at her as she swiveled toward him with indignity. It took her a moment of deep breaths to calm the seething anger she felt.

"Good, good," came a garbled chuckle from the other side. "Meet me at our second backup rendezvous in two hours. And I don't expect any delays Keto." An icy silence followed before the video feed blinked out.

Keto and the gang rose together and began exiting the room, shuffling Astrid along with them. "Hey! Just what do you think you are doing? You can't treat me like this!" Astrid became more and more frantic as Faraz once again seized her and carried her out of the airlock under his arm. Astrid continued to kick and scream as the group trooped straight down the stairs and aboard the SEA-Sparrow *Altair* that was parked in the middle of the dock. The airlock on the cramped spaceship clicked shut.

"Shh, shh, shh. Calm down. Everything is okay," Keto said, holding Astrid's head.

Astrid's head sprung up, her eyes still a little damp in the corners but smiling a guilty smile. "You think he bought it?" she said sunnily.

"Yes, my dear. That was quite a performance," Keto said as he reached out to hold Astrid's hands. She blinked away her tears and her eyes steeled thinking about how they were going to get even with the man on the other end of that line.

I can't wait to bust that sick, misogynistic bastard.

"Tell me again why there are cameras all over this loading dock?" Astrid asked. "It is because this is his loading dock. Our patron wants your samples more than anything apparently, even enough to kidnap you and reproduce your work." Keto led her by both of her hands to sit on a bench lining one side of the ship's main hold.

"I was always kept in the dark of his plans. All I knew at first was that I was supposed to rendezvous with an 'employee' of his in Earth-orbit and return. It turned out that that 'employee' was some kind of mole who tried to kill you."

"How do you know about that?"

"Colonel Mazar was kind enough to explain it to us, after a few frightening minutes looking down the barrel of a Space Marine's rifle, of course." Keto smiled reassuringly to Astrid, but behind his surface smile there was exhaustion and sadness.

"Mazar was not interested in us. We were pawns in this. He was after the mastermind - our patron."

"Can't we just leave and have Mazar take care of this?"

"We have one last part to play, I'm afraid my dear." Keto hit a transmitter on the wall behind him and said, "Are we ready?"

A voice came rattling through the speaker, "ready for liftoff." In a joking tone, the voice continued, "Ladies and gentlemen, this is your captain speaking. We will be departing shortly, please ensure your safety harness is secure and that all luggage is stowed safely in the overhead compartment."

"Timon. . .," Keto muttered under his breath, snickering.

After a moment or two of a building whine, the bay doors of loading dock opened and a small crate that was left on the floor was instantly sucked out of the opening. When the vacuum had equalized with the dock, a few loud clanks were heard before the ship itself began to undulate gently - the docking clamps had been released.

Again the smirking voice came through the speaker, "Next stop, Transfer Station T."

*   *   *   *

Mazar stared at a complex series of screens, arrayed in front of him in a half-dome, consuming his vision. After a couple of quick keystrokes on one of the data entry pads, he swiveled his chair out of the work station and popped up.
He was on the bridge of the Falconer VC-1 *Dragoon*. It was the same ship that he had witnessed the Space Marines disembarking from earlier. This was the most common deployment vehicles that the extra-orbital policing services utilized. It was fast, maneuverable, had plenty of firepower and could hold an entire platoon of Space Marines.

"As soon as we get the green light, we move in and take these traitors," Mazar announced to the command crew, spread throughout the room.
There were two pilot officers in the nose cone, tucked into a corner of the bridge. There were also two other military liaison officers. Jerek, a Staff Sergeant who was young and eager but also fiercely professional, was there to direct communication. The other was Ed Cappel, Gunnery Sargeant, who happened to be an old friend of Mazar's from boot camp. He was in his mid-forties, with a grizzled face and grey hair starting to show. He was there to direct onboard systems on the Falconer itself.

"Yes, sir," both liaison officers replied. They went back to work organizing their individual tasks while Mazar continued to monitor the progress of his screens.
On Mazar's right, a screen showed raw numbers of inventory, right above three different displays, showing first-hand images from the Space Marine's armor rigs loaded below. All they could see was the metal of the cargo hold and a small porthole window, through which only the blackness of space was visible. On the central monitor, a map showed the N-2 quadrant of the Moon and its space. A red blip was moving toward the outer rim, where two different transfer stations were located.

"Where are you heading?" Mazar mumbled to himself, rubbing the day-old fuzz on his face.

He widened another window on his left to include all of the local spacecraft in the area of the two transfer stations, and then narrowed it by cross-referencing any ships inbound to either one of the two stations. His list was down to four craft, but the way they were spread across the quadrant made it impossible to begin the interception. If he guessed wrong, and it was one of the ships on the other side, they could be out of range before he got turned around. Mazar slumped back in his chair heavily, resigned to wait a little while longer until the solution to his problem presented itself.

He had never had an assignment go this wrong before. Granted, he had achieved all of his primary objectives, but he had lost the project manager who had been slated for reenlistment on this project and was going to be sent on to Mars for the next phase of the botanical adaptation. Now, it seemed that Errol would be filling that role.

Instead, Astrid deserted with those wild men, and now they were delivering her right into the enemy's hands. He was supposed to be protecting her and she had ended up with the enemy. Luckily, they had been tracking the Toureg's ship since their first encounter and now they were leading him right to his target.

I know I'm gambling with her life, but it's the only way I can get to the bottom of this mess. Do not fear Astrid, I am coming for you.

"All right, here we go." Mazar perked up. A vector-change alert had popped up to indicate that the final approach of the Tuareg's ship had been decided; they were heading to Transfer Station T.

"I'm sending you our approach line now," Mazar said, leaning around his monitor array to get a clear line to the pilots.

"Flight path received, Colonel." One of the pilot officers responded. The *Dragoon* unclamped from the port dock and drifted in a lazy curve upwards before the topside attitude thrusters fired to level the ship off. Once the engine nozzles were safely pointing away from the surface of the Moon, the ship exploded into action. The twin pulse engines shed glistening contrails in their wake as the *Dragoon* tore off into space.

The ship boosted for a full minute straight into perfect darkness before shutting down the launch engines, and switching over to sustained thrust. Off to the right of the *Dragoon*, their destination Transfer Station T loomed in the distance.
It was a smaller installation out of the many Transfer Stations situated in the orbit of the Moon. Transfer stations generally were a kind of rest stop for emergency stops and layovers, but they did not host many facilities for long stays. This particular Transfer Station housed about 40 full-time resident employees and ran only four airlock-docks.

"We'll be approaching from the outer limits, coming out of the sun. Deploy Alpha Squad at my mark." A pause followed, until the Falconer reached its target. "Now."

Out of the portside hatch, four humanoid shapes were fired like torpedoes, speeding towards the distant station. With that, the Falconer began to swing around so that it was following the advance guard it had just deployed.

"Let's get the scramble lock up." Mazar opened a channel to the whole ship and his voice boomed over the PA, "going dark."

All over the ship, the power wound down. The only lights left on were a few running lights and the work station monitors. The three men sat in the partial darkness with the eerie blue glow from the monitors shining on their faces.

The wing, visible through the portside window, flickered and became semi-transparent. The cloaking field had kicked on. The visible spectrum cloaking was efficient but this was merely one element of masking the ship's signature.

The scramble lock eliminated the chatter that ships project for navigation and collision avoidance, with the sometimes-helpful-but-usually-annoying side effect of preventing outbound transmissions. Without these signals, the space traffic monitoring system would not be able to identify the ship.

Most scans only took a cursory look of the deep black of space because there were no other objects from which to detect a backwash or resonant signature. This made masking a ship much easier in the vast emptiness of open space.
Half of Mazar's screens were dark now, but the residual vector tracking that was running off of the ships own internal calculus showed that they were right on track.

*　　*　　*　　*

"You are clear to dock at Gate 3," the voice came over the transmitter to Timon. He fired the retro-boosters on the front of the *Altair* and glided into position.

"Are you ready?" Keto said turning to Astrid.

"As ready as I'll ever be."

The group consisted of Faraz and Khalil leading, and Timon and Keto escorting Astrid behind them. They all stepped forward through the airlock door in the back of their SEA-Sparrow into the flex-tube that spanned the gap between the ship and the station. The gravity from the ship began to fade in the flex-tube and the group bounded forward the four or five meters to the other side until the station's gravity wells brought their booted steps back to normal.

Faraz ducked into the chamber on the other side first, bending almost in half to fit through the station's airlock door. He straightened on the other side and after a brief hesitation he gestured them forward with a wave of his hand at his back. Khalil locked a semi-automatic rifle and slid through next to Faraz in a kneeling position. He popped up and stepped aside from the opening for the remaining three to enter.

The room was a lounge, though sparsely decorated. It had rows of bench seats arranged in aisles with a wide walkway down the middle. A group of three men stood on the far side of the room, shoulder to shoulder, obscuring the view into the hallway beyond and the rest of the station.

"Welcome, Thaggaren Keto," the man in the middle said, addressing Keto by his title. He was the man of rank here, wearing red on his eppelets rather than nothing.
"I am Saulters."

"Thank you. We have brought what my Patron has requested. May we see him?"

"I have instructions to take custody of Dr. Nielsen upon your arrival." Saulters paused, "I'm sorry."

Keto seized this opportunity to step forward into the man's face. "Are you telling me I came all the way up here and I can't even claim the honor of delivering this prize to my Patron myself?"

Saulters was taken aback, looking from side to side for help from either of his two henchmen. Both of them returned the blandest of looks to him.

"Yes, um, yes of course. Where are my manners?" Saulters seized Keto's hand and said, "you may accompany us to the *Astral Lance*."

Keto simply stared at him in annoyance, and the man let his hand go and turned to lead the swelling group down the corridor. Keto fell to the back covertly grabbing Timon by the arm until they were the last ones in line. He whispered "Stay with the ship and secure our escape." Timon faded away from the group with none of their hosts the wiser.

The two guards seemed to be guarding Faraz as more of a prisoner than Astrid, with one on either side of him. Saulters walked several paces ahead of them and then Astrid, Khalil and Keto brought up the rear.

After several turns and half-floor ramps, they arrived in a large boarding area. The layout was similar to the boarding area whey they had docked but on a larger scale with much nicer amenities such as thick, burgundy carpet and long, leather bench seats. There was even a chandelier that dangled from the ceiling, spraying a brilliant yellow light across the room.

The dock was occupied by a sealed hatch the size of a barn door, where dozens of porters were running in and out loading and unloading supplies. The boarding area had three different corridors through which the porters scattered. Beside the main airlock where the *Astral Lance* sat, there was a second airlock on the left of the room for maintenance crews.

Saulters led them up to the mouth of the cargo bay and turned to the Tuaregs,

"This is the *Astral Lance*, Juggernaut-class deep space cruiser."

Chapter 8

The Tuaregs stood on the loading dock staring into the cavernous cargo bay of the space cruiser before them. It was a tremendous space over a hundred feet tall, with the walls honeycombed with chambers and catwalks criss-crossing every which way.

Two guards stepped in to separate Astrid from her Tuareg entourage. Faraz and Khalil both looked to Keto for instruction, who only beckoned them to go and sit in the far corner of the boarding lounge. The guards took Astrid aboard the giant ship and Keto turned to follow her new detail.

A strange thought crossed Astrid's mind.

What if there isn't some grand scheme to rescue us? What if Keto just told me what I wanted to hear to get me here and now he really is going to slave me out?

The man who had escorted the entourage, Saulters, put a hand on Keto's chest as he reached the threshold of the massive airlock doors. "I'm sorry, but no unauthorized personnel is allowed on this ship," as two new guards coalesced from the darkness behind him.

Keto strained his eyes to look past this man into the cargo bay of the ship, and take in every detail. There against the far wall, occluded in shadow, was the man whom Keto had only met once before.

The first time Keto had met his Patron was in Pirate Town. He had looked like a humble merchant then, with his shaggy hair and dusty travelling jacket. He introduced himself as Mr. Black and Keto had never been able to get his real name. He had come to Pirate Town then to find someone to smuggle goods for him. He looked much different now, wearing a dark grey military uniform with a white collar and high, glossy black boots.

"Sir. Sir!" Keto cried over Saulters's shoulder. "Please sir, I only want to claim the honor that is mine."

Mr. Black looked up to spot Keto as he crossed the cargo bay to greet his prisoner, Astrid.

"Well, well. Our little scientist finally arrives," chuckled Mr. Black.

"You sick fuck, you're not going to get away with this." Astrid struggled against the two guardsmen's arms, and was lifted her feet off the ground. She used this opportunity to kick at Mr. Black's head, who casually knocked her leg aside.

"Why do you think I'm going to help a kidnapper like you?" Astrid asked with a note of swelling hatred in her voice.

"Well it's either that or help no one ever again," he said with an icy stare. Astrid recoiled as if stung, and started fiercely flailing against the two guards, who were now struggling to contain her.

"Sir. Sir!" Keto interjected. "Allow me to help. I have built a rapport with the woman and I believe that I may be able to help achieve cooperation."

Mr. Black watched Astrid rage against the two guards, freeing an arm and raking one of them deeply across the face with her nails. The guard yelled and let go of her waist, as the other one put her into a full nelson. She continued to buck, and stomped on the second guard's foot, who hopped about but did not release his hold.

"Alright, settle her down if you think you can. Last thing I need is one more headache." Mr. Black said, clutching the bridge of his nose.

Keto pushed past the escort and grabbed the guard constraining her by the shoulder. He eyed the newcomer dubiously before releasing Astrid. She dropped to the floor, sobbing and heaving from her knees. Keto dropped down next to her to pat her on the back.

Astrid's breathing began to slow and she looked up at Mr. Black. "Why, why are you doing this to me?"

Mr. Black took in this little scene and said, "Be a good girl and I'll explain it to you. I promise."

Keto and Astrid huddled together as Astrid gathered her wits.

"I've arranged a cabin for you. Why don't you go there and clean up for now and

I will come to talk to you later."

Keto hauled the weak-kneed Astrid back to her feet, and they shuffled past Mr. Black, following Saulters once again, this time through the long corridors of the *Astral Lance*. The main hallways ran parallel through the entire length of the ship and were wide and tall enough to drive a tank through. Every several hundred feet or so, the group crossed through giant bulkheads.

Saulters finally turned to open a door on the right side of the corridor. Through the door there was a narrower corridor and at the end of that, a gigantic chamber with vaulted ceilings. The room could easily fit a small house. It was garishly decorated in deep reds and purples with gold tassels and adornments. On one wall there was a forty-foot long window staring out into the deep, black oblivion. Another massive chandelier hung over the table in the center of the room.

Jeez. This guy really likes his chandeliers.

"You keep an eye on her, okay" Saulters said, elbowing Keto in the ribs.

He returned his best fake smile and Saulters left.

"Now all we can do is wait," Keto said.

"Don't worry. I know this guy, he'll come," Astrid replied.

*   *   *   *

"Oh, this is gooood." Colonel Mazar mumbled as he sat, soaking up information from the half dozen screens that still had data flowing in. Mazar had been doing his research on his target on top of what he already knew.

It was common knowledge that there were only eleven *Juggernaut-class* deep space cruisers originally commissioned as part of the Martian expansion. They ferried necessary building materials and start-up goods to each of the eleven colony-cities on Mars. Once the colonies were established these vessels acted as a trade fleet between the two worlds. Nothing as big had been built since.

The ships were giant cities floating in space with a skeleton crew of three hundred. They were not designed for atmospheric entry, but rather were constructed in space and constrained to stay there. The absence of the heat shielding necessary for atmospheric entry allowed these massive frigates to travel far and fast.

Each one was leased to one the eleven charter corporations that sponsored colonies on Mars. They were conceived to ferry raw and manufactured goods from Earth's orbit to Mars for as cheaply as possible. This particular one, the *Astral Lance*, was leased to Calio Systems Corporation. This company was one of the first corporations to be offered a contract from the World Order for a Mars colony installation, because they designed and manufactured self-insulated structures that were necessary for colonization purposes. They were a logical choice for one of the original contracts.

"Ah, here it is..." Mazar thought. "Audy Percorran. CEO of Calio Systems Corporation. Wealthy. Ambitious. And stupid."

It made perfect sense. He ordered the labs at Transgenix destroyed, tried to kill Astrid and steal her seed samples. Then, when he failed in that attempt, he kidnapped her to secure a monopoly on Martian-viable florae.

"Between all of the criminal acts for which Audy Percorran was accountable, we should be able to put this guy in jail for good." Mazar thought.

"Got you." Mazar snarled inaudibly.

Now that they were within range of the plethora of signals and data streams that all orbital facilities emit, several other screens came to life. One showed all of the communications bandwidths and monitored the tone and frequency of transmissions. Another generated a three dimensional map of the sector, with their own ship superimposed on the information that the station provided. The station had not scanned them yet.

Mazar always got antsy before the heat of battle. Everyone does, but he was always able to channel this nervous energy into action, swift and deliberate.

"What do we have going on?" Mazar asked Jerek.

"Alpha Squad has deployed the relay and will make contact in less than five minutes."

"Let's get the Dogs and Ponies into position."

On the two screens showing the inactive squads of Space Marines, the hatches popped open and the vantage of the two squad leaders floated out into open space. The hiss of the attitude thrusters could barely be heard as the men slowly sauntered into position. After a minute or two, the eight Marines had spread out over a cubic mile and began closing in.

"All right. Ed, is the EMP ready?"

"Yes, sir. Ready to fire when you are," Ed replied.

Mazar stood at his station, giddy with excitement. "EMP on my mark. Three, two, one. FIRE!"

A giant blue comet shot out towards the *Astral Lance.* All of the communications channels spiked as the crew of the space cruiser snapped awake. The EMP pulse slammed directly into three of the six engines. The arcs of electromagnetic current surged throughout the entire ship and many of the thousand lights flickered and went out.

Turrets on the topside of the ship popped up and were firing off into space where Alpha had deployed the communications relay. The two squads of Marines floating out in space, Dog Squad and Pony Squad began to systematically eradicate these turrets. The rain of bullets to the rear quadrant of the *Astral Lance* lit brilliant red flashes of metal on metal, dotted lines of bullet holes shredding across the gun emplacements.

Auto-targeting for the turrets used traces on weapon's inbound targeting. And since Mazar and the crew of the Falconer were sending all of their targeting information through the relay stationary satellite, the *Astral Lance* was returning fire to a target no bigger than two feet across.

Sometimes Mazar just loved his job.

*   *   *   *

Astrid and Keto sat together in their opulent prison, staring out of the bay window. The deep black of space was overwhelming to look at, to know that the only thing between you and the endless void was a four inch thick piece of glass.
The door chimed down the hallway as it slid open and Mr. Black strode through.

"As promised, here I am," he said in a pissy way, as if he thought he should be commended for keeping his commitment.

Mr. Black sat in the chair at the head of the room and templed his fingers in front of his face. He considered the pair before him for a moment or two before beginning. "This wasn't supposed to go down the way it did. I never meant for anyone to get hurt. All I wanted were your seeds. You have a lab full of those seeds back on Earth don't you? So what's the big deal about me taking a look?"

Realizing the statement sounded like a justification, Mr. Black took another tact. "Listen. I operate Cidade de Montanha, the colony on Mars. Those seeds could be used to change the lives of my citizens. We could make Mars just like Earth, but instead they are stuck in committee on how to *best implement the greater terra-forming strategy*.

That technology could be used now."

"Aren't they studying the projected long-term effects of a total reconstruction of a planet for human habitation?" Keto burst out.

Mr. Black glared openly at him and Keto stared right back in open defiance. Mr. Black was taken aback, as Astrid leaned forward to whisper in Keto's ear.

"It's all bullshit. I don't have the seed samples with me and Transgenix would never let me back into the building. It would take years to recreate my work. His only motive here is money. He wants to privatize Mars' terra-forming. And let me tell you, this is not something that you leave to free markets."

"What is this lovefest?" Mr. Black yells, standing red-faced out of his chair.

Just then an alarm klaxon sounded, and a barely understandable voice came on over the P.A. "Captain to the bridge, all hands to their stations. Captain to the bridge, all hands to their stations."

Mr. Black cursed and ran for the door. "Don't you go anywhere now. You're the whole reason I'm in this mess!"

"YOU'RE the whole reason you're in this mess!" Astrid shrieked after him.

Mr. Black turned to leave and locked the hallway door as it slid closed.

A second later a huge blast rocked the entire room, as the chandelier's crystals clinked together like raindrops. Then, all of the lights went out one by one before the red glow of the emergency lights blinked on.

"Look, it knocked the power out. Now's our chance to make a break for it," Keto said, turning to Astrid who was sitting on a big, purple couch on one side of the room. "If we can get back to the *Altair* and make our escape, Mazar won't follow us. He has what he wanted."

"What, run away like cowards?" Astrid replied sitting up straighter. "When we risked our lives to help them uncover this conspiracy? Don't we deserve some credit."

"I do not think that he will see it like that, my dear. The Colonel may very well feel obligated to bring you back to fulfill his directive. The classified nature of your research creates the possibility that they will not let you out of your service contract." Keto began pacing back and forth in front of Astrid. "They could send you on to Mars, next. You said yourself that that was what would be required of the project manager. Is that what you want?"

"I thought I did, at one point. But now, I don't know. I think I want to be where I can help real people, with real problems right now. I am all for the colonization project, but it is too abstract for me. I put my time in, made my contributions, but it's not for me anymore. Errol will be a great project manager. The three days we spent working on that presentation had me believing he knew more about my research than I did," Astrid rambled, then paused a moment in silent reflection before continuing. "What am I saying? Of course he knew more about my research than I did. He actually got the memory implant."

"Sounds like we both want the same thing," Keto said, pulling a long, thin dagger from his many layers. Keto loomed over Astrid in the semi-darkness, the pale red glow from the emergency lights shining on his face in a sinister way. He walked toward her, seeming to grow larger and more menacing as he approached. With a breath of relief, Astrid realized that he was simply approaching the door to the hallway when he sidled past her.

He walked over to the door and slid the blade between the two sealed halves of the door and began dragging it up and down. The blade caught on something unseen, and with a little jiggling, the blade slid through the door up to the hilt. Keto leveraged the two sides against each other enough to get a handhold on the door and slide it back manually.

"After you, my dear." Keto flourished to Astrid as she smoothed her linen pants while standing.

"I really should start trusting you more, considering you've never been anything but a true gentleman to me," Astrid said to him, as she brushed past through the partially obstructed doorway.

*   *   *   *

The barrage of fire continued, as some of the turrets were redirected toward the two squads of heavily armed and armored Marines. Their super- heavy caliber rounds bit hole after hole into the thick metal on the stern of the *Astral Lance.* One of the turrets still firing out into space at the relay satellite got lucky and blew away the decoy.

Suddenly, the targeting systems throughout the Falconer and all of the Marine armor rigs went screwy.

"Ed, redirect the targeting computer to direct feed," Mazar said.

The man typed frantically and the data stream resumed its flood of information into the system. The two screens on which Mazar was monitoring the Dogs and Ponies shimmered and the right margin began to fill with targeting and tactical data once again.

The remaining turrets on the *Astral Lance* were aimed at the sector where the Marines were located. Random flares of the Marines' thruster packs flashed as the tracers from the turret occasionally chased a Marine from his spot. The Marines nevertheless continued the bombardment, eviscerating one turret after another, leaving smoldering holes in their fire's wake.

"Hold 'em off just a little longer boys," Mazar intoned through the channel to these two squads.

*   *   *   *

"We're making entry." *Pshht.* The comm channel hissed shut. Lance Corporal Baum of Alpha Squad floated fifty feet or so away with his two squadmates, Gumby and Deuce. PFC Weggeller was setting a charge on the hull of the *Astral Lance*. It towered over them hundreds of feet, a sheer wall of metal. Baum liked this spot because there were no portholes within three hundred feet of his squad, no prying eyes to send up an early signal. Far above and on the other side of this behemoth ship, the distinct whispers of gunfire could be heard.

Wegeller raised his rig's booted legs and kicked off of the hull. His vector took him right for the rest of the squad before he swung his legs around and fired his attitude thrusters to negate his momentum. A moment later, a loud, short pop was immediately silenced by the vastness of space and a cloud of debris was forced in all directions as the air was sucked out.

The Marines filed into their entry and settled on the floor of the now-defunct hydraulics room. "Open her up," Baum said to another one of the Marines, Gumby, who stepped forward to crack the control panel. The fingers of his suit worked fluidly and delicately across the circuit underneath and the door slid open. The Marines immediately stormed through the door to take up a defensive two-and-two position in the hallway.

Baum waved the door shut from the other side and the air pressure equalized, but the alarm klaxons continued to blare.

"All clear!" Weggeler said from the other side.

"Let's move it out!" Baum said and began stomping down the corridor. They got about a hundred feet from their target when a dozen armed guards trooped around the corner. "Two down, two down!" Baum shouted and he and Gumby dropped to one knee and Weggeller and Deuce stood over them to create a wall of firepower.

The guards, obviously stunned at the amount and size of firearms aimed at them, slowed and as some of them tried to take cover in shallow doorways, others tried to urge the charge on.

"Drop your weapons!" Baum shouted into his megaphone, his voice booming down the hallway.

A guard with a grenade launcher stepped up in front of the milling crowd and fired. As it whizzed down the hallway at Alpha Squad, Gumby sprayed chaff from his gun in front of them and the grenade exploded, lightly pelting the squad with debris.

"Gel slugs. Let's drop'em!" Baum said and flipped a switch to fire the non-lethal ammunition in his gun.

At this point half the guards were scattering down the hall, and the others were firing pistols and submachine guns. A barrage of gel slugs covered the hallway, ricocheting off of walls and bodies, until all of the guards slumped to the ground.

"Move out," Baum said and rallied his squad forward. Once they got to the mounds of unconscious bodies, the squad had to shuffle through them so as not to crush one of them under the powerful, hydraulic legs of the suit. Once through the quagmire of bodies, the squad double-timed it to their destination: the bridge.

Baum used a finger camera in his suit to peer around the corner where another detail of armed guards stood at the ready. These guards had armor vests and high-powered assault rifles; the elite, they were dressed in dark blue high-collar uniforms with black tabs.

"I guess we're gonna have to get nasty," Baum said

Deuce smiled a wide, toothy grin and says, "Let's get nasty." Deuce spun around the corner and dropped to one knee. His suit has a special shield built into the right arm, so that the barrel of his gun and the face of the shield were practically all the target could see.

"Freeze!" Deuce shouted. Immediately, the guards shift into a defensive position behind makeshift bunkers of overturned furniture and crates stacked in the hallway. The guards fired down the hallway and two bullets deflect off of the side of Deuce's head.

"Fuckin' warned 'em." Deuce growled as he fired an incendiary grenade down the hall toward the three clusters of guards. The grenade skipped and skittered until it sat in the middle of all three temporary bunkers. It exploded in jets of flame in all directions, consuming the hallway with fire for a second or two. The men in the two forward bunkers flailed in agony or slumped to the floor. The third bunker had one man with a small fire burning on his sleeve which could barely be seen from behind their cover. He quickly patted it out.

"Take the lead, Deuce. Stack attack." Baum said and as Deuce stood, Baum fell in behind him pointing his rifle around Deuce's shoulder. The rest of the squad fell in line in the same way, single file down the hallway. "Come out with your hands up, I'm not fucking around anymore!" Baum yelled through his megaphone.

The five men left camping behind the last bunker finally stood with their hands up, covered in soot and one of them a little toasted. The burnt one was still holding a pistol in his raised hand as Deuce walked up to him and stuck his forty-two pound, 9.5 caliber rail gun directly in his face. The arachnid eyes of the armor rig stared down the barrel of the gun as Deuce's booming, ominous voice said, "What're you gonna do with that little peashooter? Huh?"

The elite guard visibly trembled and dropped the pistol.

"Thought so," Deuce said, and clubbed the man unconscious with the butt of his gun.

The bridge blast-doors stood in front of them. These were the most heavily armored doors as they protected the nerve center of the ship. But both of their objectives lay behind those doors. One, take Audy Percorran, aka Mr. Black, CEO of Calio Systems Corporation into custody. And two, decommission the *Astral Lance*.

"Open the doors now or you risk getting burned when we cut through it." Baum said in a cool voice through the megaphone.

After a moment or two, the blast doors slid back and then the heavy, airlock doors retracted. Audy Percorran was standing in the doorway, in his dark grey uniform with a white collar. "Audy Percorran, I am taking you into the custody of the World Order for treason."

Chapter 9

       Dog Squad leader waved the detachment to cease fire. The cessation of all fire seemed eerily calm as the eight Marines floated in the deep space. The Falconer *Dragoon* phased into sight directly behind them, several miles from the transfer station where the deep space cruiser was at port. The turrets on the *Astral Lance* had all been eviscerated by long, jagged, bullet-riddled scars up and down the ship's topside. From this distance, the red glow of the emergency lights made the behemoth look angry, with thousands of beady, red eyes staring.

Mazar walked over to Jerek's communications console behind the two pilot officers of the Falconer. He picked up the microphone and turned to Jerek.

       "Do we have comm back up?" Mazar asked, and Jerek nodded affirmative.

       "Alpha, what's your status?" Mazar said into the microphone, after Jerek keyed open the channel.

       "Alpha here. We are currently in the process of decommissioning the target, we have Aces in hand." Baum's voice scratched over the channel.

       "Good work, Lance Corporal. Hold there, we're on our way." Mazar said into the mic, then turned to Jerek and said, "Round 'em up. We're going in."

       The Dog and Pony squads began to swarm back to the Falconer, their backs lit with the incandescent glow of the ion repulsors like lightning bugs. They disappeared underneath the massive wingspan of the plane.

The *Dragoon* accelerated once again and took a long arc to park in the remaining airlock on Transfer Station T, observing the damage they had wrought on the titanic cruiser. The rear quadrant had borne the brunt of the attack, with four of the six massive engines smoldering vapors into space from myriad cracks in their containment shells. The top of the Astral Lance had been shredded precisely with long trails of craters from the Marine's gunfire criss-crossing the many now-defunct turrets. The EMP had burned out most of the electrical systems, leaving only the red glow shining out of the many portholes.

The *Dragoon* coasted into the last remaining airlock on Transfer Station T. Mazar beckoned Jerek and Ed to follow him as he left the bridge of the Falconer and bounded down the narrow hallway and narrower stair to the hold below. In a small cargo area that was not cordoned off with the Marine's airlocks, Keen and Harpo sat, waiting.

"You two come with me," Mazar said walking through the cargo area toward the docking airlock. He looked through the porthole to see that the seal was in place, and opened the door to a warm, stale breeze.

The group proceeded forward into their boarding lounge and on through into the hallways of the transfer station. Mazar walked like a man possessed, with the rest of the entourage having to trot or jog to keep up.

They reached the *Astral Lance*. The boarding lounge was complete chaos. Benches had been tossed over each other to form long rows of cover, behind which half a dozen men crouched. They were well armed and armored, all wearing the same uniform, a dark blue with black collars and eppelets.

When they saw Mazar and his group these guards immediately began to fire. Ed Cappel and Mazar burst into action, sprinting forward and dive-rolling to cover on either side of the doorway. Mazar was flat on his belly behind a bullet-proof munitions crate and Ed kneeled behind a large plant, potted in a steel drum.

"You are firing on Officers of the Law!" Mazar yelled over the din of the firearms.

"Get them down here," Mazar said over his shoulder to Jerek, squinting as bullets ricocheted around him.

The other three peeled back from the doorway to take cover around the corners. As Harpo ran around Jerek to get to cover, a bullet hit him in the foot and a light spray of blood covered the wall. He stumbled and fell to his knees and drags himself around the corner.

"I'm hit!" Harpo yelled.

Mazar heard this and saw red. A guard sprayed the pot Ed was hiding behind with his automatic rifle, standing a mere ten feet away with a bloodthirsty look in his eye. Mazar took careful aim with his Blackfoot .50 caliber handgun, and put a slug in the guard's temple.

Keen from behind the corner, sprayed the tops of the overturned benches with his rifle and another of the guards screamed and clutched his face. Metal fragments from the bench splintered off and sprayed him with shrapnel.

"Cease fire in the name of the New World Order!" Mazar yelled, attempting a detente.

The guards did not stop firing, but instead concentrated on Mazar's position. A sudden pressure change in the room and the clanging of the exterior airlock opening behind them made all of the guards turn to see what was going on. Out of the door came two Dog Squad Space Marines.

One of the now-panicked guards began firing his rifle at the Marines while the other three behind the nearest bench froze, dropping their guns. The Marine furthest from Mazar and company shot one round from his massive rail gun which hit the guard on his trigger hand. The blowback was tremendous as the guard's gun was ripped apart like a wax replica. The guard was tossed back and slammed against the far wall five feet above the ground before crumpling into a bloody heap.

Mazar stood and said "Take them to the station mess hall."

The Marine nodded and began prodding the three prisoners back toward the mess hall on Transfer Station T. The airlock slid open again as the rest of Dog Squad trooped through and Mazar rounded everyone up.

"All right. We need to sweep this ship for any more of these resistors. Pony is taking the aft side of the ship and we have Alpha holding down the bridge."
Harpo limped forward to join them. "Harpo, I need you to hunker down here and make sure no one gets out. Don't be a hero. Call it in if there's too many." Mazar turned back to address the group. "Remember, we're dealing with almost a hundred armed soldiers between security and enforcement. Jerek, you and I are taking Dog Four and heading for the bridge. Dog One and Two, go with Keen and Ed and search the fore ship."

Mazar and Jerek flanked either side of their Marine escort as the trio strode down the main corridor towards the bridge.

*   *   *   *

Astrid and Keto ran through the wide corridors of the Astral Lance back the way they came with the man Saulters. They ran crouched over in a vain attempt to conceal themselves, though they had yet to encounter anyone else in these halls.

Keto led the way down the long corridors. At one point, he stopped in his tracks and pushed Astrid into a shallow doorway. The shuffling sound of footsteps began to echo through the dim red-washed corridor louder now. Keto risked putting his hand out to wave the door open and the two of them fell through to a connecting corridor between the two main passageways that extended the length of the ship. The door slid shut silently and the clamor of footsteps was silenced.
Keto helped Astrid to her feet as they ran down the intersecting corridor to the other side of the ship. He waved this door open and peered around the corner before snapping back to the hallway pressing Astrid back.

The door slid shut again and Keto held his finger up to his mouth to indicate silence. He pressed his ear to the door as more drumming bootsteps pounded past. A minute passed before Keto ventured back out into the central corridor.

"That was a close one. We need to get back to the ship."

The pair continued down the main corridor, hugging the walls. The corridor took them back to the massive cargo bay, tucked into the nose of the ship. The airlock connected to Transfer Station T and freedom was a hundred meters away. Keto hunkered down as they reached the final bulkhead before the cavernous cargo bay. It seemed clear at first glance, but he caught movement out of the corner of his eye along the far wall.

Keto led Astrid around the corner quickly to hide behind a stack of random crates in the corner. He risked another look over their new cover and saw the movement was a soldier in solid green fatigues, who was now shuffling forward baring an automatic rifle, crouched in a shoot-ready position.

From another corner, a burst echoed from another gun clattering around the soldier's form, who rolled behind crates to take cover from the new direction. He stood and returned fire to the spot the muzzle had flared, and then began to approach the new target by weaving between crates.

Cszzz "I got shots fired down here, need back-....."

A bone-crunching sound rang out as a giant shape spear-tackled the advancing soldier from behind his crate cover.

"All clear," Khalil's heavily accented voice rasped loudly. He stepped forward with his semi-automatic rifle from behind his cover to advance to the downed soldier. Faraz the beast stood and shouldered the soldier's weapon.

Keto and Astrid stood and trotted over to the airlock door. "We don't have much time now. Let's move."

The Tuaregs and Astrid fled through the nightmarish main boarding lounge, covered with streaks of blood and piles of corpses. The walls were riddled with bullets and the great chandelier overhead had been splintered into a thousand shards of glass scattered everywhere. Navigating the piles of chairs and crates strewn about, they reached the hallway and broke into a sprint back toward the SEA-Sparrow and safety.

*   *   *   *

Mazar stood on the bridge of the *Astral Lance*. It was a massive chamber with windows covering the entirety of three of the walls. The various control stations were sunk into the chamber floor with a central dais, rising in the middle.

In one corner, Weggeler the Alpha Squad Marine stood corralling the technicians normally stationed throughout the bridge. Gumby, the remaining Marine was crouched down in his suit, interfacing with a series of forward controls. The head of his suit was folded back, and the shoulders were slumped to either side of his chest. He was leaning forward typing fiercely on three different keyboards in front of him. In front of Mazar stood Audy Percorran, framed on either side with the Marines, Baum and Deuce.

"You certainly have made an awful mess for me to clean up," Mazar spat at Percorran through clenched teeth.

"It was the right thing to do," Audy said, raising his chin defiantly. "I have real lives depending on me, depending on a green Mars. If I have to go to jail because of that dream, then so be it."

"Drop the act. You and I both now you don't give a damn about your settlers, Audy. The recent covert statistics regarding Martian cities came out the other day. Maybe you'd like to read them." Mazar brandished a clear panel that flexed as he waved it back and forth.

"*Cidade de Montanha has the lowest overall approval ratings in all of the key indicators except for industrial output...* yada yada." Mazar trailed off reading and picked up again where the article returned to relevancy. "*Wide areas of the city have been given over to organized crime families who hold a familial relationship with the sponsoring corporation. It is clear that these gangs are used as brute squads both in this city but also to intimidate and attack neighboring interests.*"

Mazar stopped to look up at Audy, who was still staring defiantly forward. "That is one man's opinion. Only living there, being born there could one know the truth of the situation." Audy had disdain for this interpretation leaking into his voice.

"It's clear to me what your motive is, Audy. You obviously have a vast financial interest in keeping the settlers out there on the Red Planet encapsulated. Calio

Systems Corporation is heavily vested in seeing the continuance of Martian habitational construction. You don't want a Green Mars. You would keep everyone under the dome forever if it was up to you. That's why you tried to kill
Dr. Nielson and destroy the seeds."

"You have no proof for these wild accusations. I have done nothing wrong." "I've already got a work-up on your assassin buddy. Seems he hails from Cidade de Montanha too," Mazar said continuing to read through the electronic dossier. "And I'm thinking that's just the beginning of the connection between you two.

The autopsy should yield some interesting results. Oh, and I forgot to mention your 'guest' downstairs. Something tells me you didn't invite her over for tea." The wheels in Audy's head began to turn at the revelation that the police already knew that Dr. Astrid Nielsen was onboard right now.

"But, but" Audy began blubbering, "can I talk to you privately?" Audy was now acutely aware that everyone in the room was staring at this exchange, save the Marines that remained vigilantly attentive to their prisoners. "I am willing to cooperate, if you will consider it during my sentencing."

A slow grin crept over Mazar's face as he considered this. "You will cooperate anyway if you know what's good for you." Mazar said, pausing to study his adversary. "Fine, let's see what you've got."

Mazar waved away the two Marines Baum and Deuce, saying "Why don't you start taking prisoners down to the mess hall on the transfer station." Mazar released his grasp to allow the prisoner to walk past him to a meeting room off of the bridge. Mazar followed closely behind as Audy entered the room and the doors snapped shut behind him.

As soon as the doors closed, Audy spun a sharp backhand into Mazar's face, which stunned him as he shrank to one knee. Audy had already hurdled the conference table and was running out of the back of the room when the spots cleared from Mazar's vision.

As soon as he could see again, he was up and running down the same narrow corridor through which his quarry had fled. It was a labyrinthine series of narrow passageways, branching off of one another. Mazar stopped running when he could no longer hear Audy's footfalls and took a different tactic.

"Gumby, close off G-Block, no exit."

Szsht. "G-Block locked down, sir."

"Now, now. I don't have time for games, Audy. Come out now and save yourself the embarrassment. There's nowhere for you to run."

Mazar continued to stealthily stalk through the halls of G-Block, pausing to listen to the subtle sounds that emanated around him. A rustling led him towards another, smaller open room. As Mazar glided around the threshold he saw Audy, with his back toward Mazar, quietly loading an automatic rifle from a weapon rack.

Mazar took two more soft steps before springing at the man. Audy heard him at the last second and turned the gun to fire. Mazar grabbed the gun as Audy squeezed off two rounds that went just wide of Mazar's head. Mazar grabbed the man's wrist and with a quick twist, splintered his carpals.

Audy made no cry of pain, but rather tried to force the barrel into Mazar's face. Mazar resisted easily and used his leverage, to overwhelm Audy's weakened grip and slam the barrel of the rifle into his nose. Audy blindingly kicked at the back of Mazar's knee as Mazar ripped the gun from the man's crippled hand. Mazar bent his leg with the kick and had to crouch slightly to avoid the force of the blow. He raised the seized rifle to parry a flurry of fists before Whipping around and cracking Audy across the face with the butt of the rifle. Audy flopped to the floor on his back, panting hard as Mazar towered over him with the rifle propped on his hip.

"You're under arrest for espionage, conspiracy to commit murder, kidnapping, grand treason and now, attempted murder. You will be transferred to the ISS for holding and eventually your trial. And if you have hurt one hair on that innocent woman's head, God help you."

Audy said nothing and stared up at him with wide, vicious eyes like that of a feral cat. Without taking his eyes off of his prisoner, Mazar called back to the bridge.

"Gumby, open up G-Block again."

"Yes sir, and the SEA-Sparrow *Altair* is releasing their docking clamps now."

Mazar stood there for a moment, contemplating. "Let them go. I got what I came here for?"

"Aye, sir." Gumby replied and the channel snapped shut.

Mazar turned back to Audy, "Now, where is this guest room?"

* * * *

Timon accelerated away from the scene of cosmic carnage, the leviathan behind them gutted like a trout and smoking into the blackness. He hadn't even asked for clearance, he had just popped the docking clamps and ran. Transfer Station T was practically abandoned when they ran full speed back to their ship. The only thing that

Timon worried about was a pursuit of some kind, but it seems that the plan worked and they had escaped unhindered.

They had escaped. He smiled as he flicked the switches to prepare for the asymptotic atmospheric re-entry that the shuttle necessitated. The Earth loomed above them as the *Altair* began to creep into the approach descent.

Behind the cockpit, Keto was laughing and clapping his male companions heartily on the shoulder. He turned to Astrid and said, "We made it! When we return, we will have a ceremony to welcome you to our tribe. But until then, I want you to wear this."

Keto held out a necklace, made from bones and polished beads, which Astrid bowed her head for, to allow Keto to place it around her neck. Looking down, she saw her other gold baguette necklace and took it off. She held it between her thumb and forefinger, rolling the gold pendant around her hand.

Astrid uncorked the top of the necklace and shook the contents of the empty, pea-pod shaped pendant into her hand. There were six clear capsules, each with half a dozen seeds inside.

"I carry these everywhere I go because they meant so much to me. Now they can mean that much to you, to us." Astrid said and delicately placed the spheres back into the golden tube. She handed the gold necklace to Keto, who had a stunned look on his face.

"If what Khalil has told me is true, this necklace could completely change our situation." Keto cupped the necklace delicately between his hands, like a flower blossom. "Thank you."

"You will really like Pirate Town, Astrid," Khalil said after an appreciative moment had passed. "It may not look like much on the surface, but it holds treasure and beauty of indefinable quality. I will have to show you the lab I have set aside and perhaps we can work together."

"Yes, I would like that a lot. I am looking forward to the whole experience."

*   *   *   *

Mazar stood in front of the hallway door to the guest room suite with Private Keen beside him. He took a deep breath and waved the door. The door slid open roughly, and Mazar marched through. Keen stood guard at the door.

"Fuck!"

Keen ran in to find Mazar, tossing the furniture in the room in a vain attempt to find the prisoner who wasn't there.

Epilogue

Astrid stood and wiped the beads of sweat from her forehead with the cloth binding her wrists. The cloth was protected from the blowing sand by her outer garment and so it was clean enough to wipe the stinging sweat from her eyes. Astrid wore a full-length dark brown jalabiya with a white scarf wrapped over her nose and mouth to shield her respiration.

She took in her handiwork. Astrid had never had an outdoor garden before and she found that toiling under the sun to care for these great plants gave her a deep sense of satisfaction. The garden she had been working on was a wide plot of hedge-rows and short, strange-looking trees encompassing a plethora of fruits and vegetable stands grown in the rich soil basin within.

Astrid had been hard at work with her partner, Khalil al-Fazzi to establish hundreds of these desert oases throughout this area of their land. With a little help from modern science, she and her Tuareg clansmen had been able to convert the unforgiving Sahara into a livable place.

This particular garden was much smaller than the others because it was next to the buried city the Tuaregs called their home. This was Pirate Town, where a handful of rooftop doorways dotted among the trees and crops were all there was to indicate there was anything more to this particular garden. Even those doors that were visible were intentionally obscured by foliage.

Astrid walked towards a copse of squat red palms that looked out of place and brushed a few fronds aside. Among a rough frame of timbers, within a mound of sand in the center, was a door. She grasped the heavy, iron ring and pulled to hoist the door open and descended within.

The hollow sand dune was actually a partially collapsed and repaired sandstone stairwell. Long ago, this had been the top of the tallest building in Pirate Town. Now, it and only a few other doors remained that allowed access to the catacombs below. As she walked down the carved stone stairs, the warm glow emanating from below grew in intensity.

After a flight of cold stone steps, a carpet runner started and escorted her down into a grand chamber. Nearly all of the chambers in Pirate Town were supported by timbers that were retrofitted to the spaces to prevent cave-ins. The rooms themselves were originally constructed from timbers but as the cave-ins continued, the walls and floors were gradually replaced by light-weight Flexcrete, a strong but flexible plastic-type building material. This allowed for tighter fitting joints to prevent sand eroding the ceiling, floors and walls.

The room in which Astrid now stood had an ancient oak dining table with silver inlay in the middle of it, as well as all kinds of historical artifacts. On one wall, was an old oil painting from a well-known artist of the 21st century and in the corner was a bronze statue of a javelineer.

She took off her outer garment, hanging it on a brass coat hanger in the corner and plopped down in one of the Victorian chairs by the oak table. She heaved a contented sigh, and began flipping through the schematics for the myriad gardens on a hand held computer. It was a simple clear panel able to display the hundreds of designs that she and Khalil had come up with.

Khalil had surprised her by being an extraordinary scientist. He was extremely intelligent and current with all of the most recent research. He had an utterly unique knowledge base built on the oral traditions of the tribe and the preserved manuscripts housed here, in the libraries of Pirate Town. He had a fully stocked laboratory down below in a converted space that used to house the Mamma Haidara Library.

Astrid finalized the plat changes she had just made in the hand-held organizer and set it down on the fine silver inlay. She stood to seek out her partner, Khalil. Astrid wandered out around a steel buttress that created one of the doorways for this room, and down another stair past the central chamber of the Great Mosque of Djingareyber. She descended the stair three flights until she was level with the great chamber's floor and turned onto the main thoroughfare through Pirate Town.

Deep below the sand, the endless catacombs stretched for miles between old hollows from mud buildings that had been swallowed by the sands. Down here, the plaza of this ancient city made up the core of their secret dwelling. As she strolled down the underground main street she was always amazed at the history and the culture this place embodied.

Many of the old facades had been saved and restored, especially here where the original excavation had taken place. The original mud architecture was more decorative than anything now, but storefronts still used the preserved spaces within for their trade and the millennia-old brass lampposts colonnading the main street still functioned, shining a warm glow throughout the plaza.

Children skirted in and around her legs, playing as she walked. Ahead, past the cluster of commerce, the old University of Sankore had been converted into a dormitory for families and tribesmen.

She turned down the last turn off of the main street into a long, narrow hallway that blasted her with air as she entered. She walked down the passage to a heavy, steel door. She turned the vault-like lock and swung the slab of a door open.
Within, she found a laboratory dressing room with a decontamination chamber and a plate glass window separating it from another room of equal size. A well-built man stood over a miniaturized bombardment chamber in the lab, staring at it through a magnifying spectacle attached to headgear, his hands planted squarely on either side.

Astrid strolled over to the plate glass window and observed Khalil at work. He had a staggering intensity about him as he stared at his experiment. The initial sequencing of Astrid's seed samples had taken them a lot of time since they had had to reverse-engineer each species. Astrid recalled enough information to speed this process along, and eventually they had reproduced all thirty six varieties.

She was especially proud of her contribution to this community. She had helped them create their own farmlands out of nothing and now their community and their culture flourished again, through trade with friendly neighbors, not through the illicit behaviors they had resorted to before.

Once the reverse engineering of her seed collection was complete, she established a nursery with Khalil and the two of them and a slew of workers from the tribe had begun planting the first round. The *profundus radix peniculus* was planted first to create an artificial water table. This plant looks like a big, round ball with a tuft of leaves on top and thick, scaly bark all around. It establishes a deep taproot down to the natural water table and then extrudes thick, spongy root branches under the sand to sprout up new offshoots which surface and start the process over again.

These spongy roots artificially elevate the water table by leaching the water they draw from deep below to underneath the surface. Once the shallower water table is established, new species are introduced which biologically convert sand and organic material to a more fertile state. *Calx epotus*, the sand swallower and *crustulum plasmator*, which breaks down the organic materials of other purposefully invasive species, are two examples of these species that transform the barren sand into usable, sandy soil.

The next stage in the transformation was to inject crucial nutrients and complete the soil conversion. Other tailor-made species performed this task admirably, using their natural photosynthesis to convert sun and water into organic matter which could be broken down and mixed with the sand to sway the equilibrium of the soil.

Protective covering to the converted acreages was established to shield the converted lands from the sweltering desert conditions of heat and wind. Hedge rows are established to buffer the growing fields from the wind and taller trees are planted around the fringe to offer shade.

They had established hundreds of these oases scattered across this part of the desert. And through this process Khalil and Astrid had learned a lot from each other and each had developed a profound respect for the other. Astrid snapped back into the present and Khalil was still in the same position, towering over his lab station.

Astrid knocked on the plate glass window, and Khalil started. He looked up and the corners of his eyes perked up in a smile, the rest of his face covered in a sterile facemask. He straightened himself out and came around the work bench to enter the decontamination chamber. After a moment or two he emerged, sloughing his lab coat and facemask.

"Hi honey," Astrid said smiling.

"Hello dear," Khalil responded leaning in to kiss her on the mouth in greeting.

"I finished the northeast city plot just now. It's already updated in the system."

"Great!" Khalil said enthusiastically. "This splice is going to take a while yet. Do you want to head up to the Eastern Slopes with me to check in on the starter beds?"

"Sure, we still have a couple hours of daylight left. Let's go."

Khalil hung up his lab coat and facemask before removing his non-permeable bodysuit and exchanging it for the traditional *salwar kemeez*. Khalil turned and grasped Astrid's hand, and they edged their way through the too-narrow vault doorway, and continued down the hallway shoulder to shoulder.

"I think Keto is already out there checking on some of the new monitoring stations he put up the other day. You know, I think he's getting more paranoid now that we're doing better," Khalil said, a tone of worry entering his voice.

"He'll be all right. He just worries so much now that we are doing so well."

The pair continued through the city to one of the underground parking garages. The wide, concrete bunker was filled with vehicles, mostly dune buggies and ATVs. Astrid swung into a newer-looking dune buggy that stood farther off of the floor due to its heavy-duty shocks. Khalil hopped in next to her and the pair looked at each other before putting on goggles and raising their scarves. The engine echoed through the garage as the buggy zipped toward the door.

The garage door was pitched out at the bottom and as it rolled up, jets of air all around the opening breathed out into the parching desert. The sand swirled around the mouth of the garage before blowing away as the deep grooves of the buggy's tires ripped into the dune.

The buggy lightly sprang over the rolling sand as it tore across the dune crests. The glaring sun was diffused into an enjoyable glow underneath the buggy's tinted roof. Far in the distance, a wide tree line sprang up behind one massive dune before another rose from the wasteland behind it. The pair could only see the leafy tips as they crested one dune and started down the next.

As they approached, the scope of the Eastern Slope was impressive. They had found a natural trench that was caused by huge, rocky outcroppings to the south. The winds generated from the Gulf of Guinea were channeled down the Niger River Valley to scour the desert. The torrents of sand could swallow an area in one day and be gone the next. But here in the shelter of the rocks, the wind had piled to shear dunes from the draft off of the rock. These two massive dunes, formed this protected canyon

Their dune buggy climbed the high crest before the verdant valley dawned before them. The narrow forest stretched for miles and miles in either direction and in the distance to the south, the rocky outcropping capping the valley. Astrid looked on to the Eastern Slopes farmland and smiled broadly. She turned to Khalil and exchanged the warm smile with him before revving up the electric buggy again and zipping south along the ridgeline toward the rocks.

The forest fell away into true farmland before a few buildings sprouted up. There was a small town established at the base of the massive rocky outcropping. This was an outpost town where they excavated from the sandstone quarry to the south and farmed the fertile valley to the north.

Astrid headed down the Eastern Slope into the quaint, little village below. She slowed down as they entered the town passing a vineyard on the left and a squat silo and a baked-clay schoolhouse to the right. The road opened into a plaza at the center of town in front of the main hall and the Excavator's Guild. Astrid stopped in the plaza and between the two buildings she could see the excavation underway. The quarry hummed with human activity and the entrance to the site was bracketed by wooden scaffolds. A short man in a vest and matching pants trotted out from the main hall towards Astrid and Khalil.

"*A Salaam a likum,* Imoshagh Al-Fazzi," the secretary greeted Khalil.

"*Waliksha a Salaam,* Rahim. Have you seen my uncle? We need to talk to him."

"Yes, he's here. He went up to the monitoring station on the Stone Fields about an hour ago."

"All right. We'll be back soon."

Rahim nodded and bowed away from the buggy. Khalil nodded at Astrid and she floored it again toward the sloping road the wound up and around a rocky face that bordered the eastern edge of the town.

"You know, people think I'm strange for letting you drive."

"Good thing we both know you don't care about that sort of thing," Astrid replied. "Besides, I think it's fun and you prefer to ride. Makes perfect sense to me."

Khalil chuckled beside her as they roared around the cliff face and under a rocky overhang before springing out into the whipping sand of the Stone Fields.
The brilliant blue of the Gulf of Guinea poked out here and there on the horizon as they passed the rocky outcropping and the sand in front of them became much rockier. The sand scoured across them and made it very hard to see, as Astrid tried to hug the edge of the barren expanse of wind-scoured stones. She popped over a dune to gain respite from the sandstorm.

In front of them a watchtower and a small hut rose from the dunes. The tower was topped with the sensor cluster, and the hut was half-buried in the sand. Astrid drove right up to the hut and saw no sign of life. Khalil and Astrid disembarked and Khalil cracked the hut door to peek inside. He waved to Astrid to come inside as he slipped into the crack. Astrid followed cracking the door only enough to slip through.

Astrid followed Khalil down a half-flight of poured concrete stairs, to the wooden floor. The hut was large compared to its exterior appearance, about ten meters in diameter, with the walls pitched inward. It had a lofted ceiling into the pitch of the roof, and a wide half-spiral stair in one corner led down to a wider, lower level.

Keto was sitting at the table in the middle of the floor, and his eyes lit up when he saw the pair. These twinkling eyes were lined heavily with wrinkles and his hair was mostly dark grey. He stood deliberately, using his arms to boost him from his seat.

"Well, this is a treat. I do not get to visit with you two enough these days." He shuffled over to embrace each of them in turn, holding them lovingly for several moments. Keto turned toward the lower level and coughed before speaking,

"Fatima, pour some tea. Astrid and Khalil are here."

The head of a beautiful young woman poked her head out from below and saw the two new arrivals. "Sure, Grandpa. Hey, you two."

"Hi Fatima," Astrid said smiling.

As Fatima retreated Astrid turned back to Keto. "She is getting more beautiful by the day."

"Yes, she is a treasure. My family grows large and it makes me so happy." Keto lowered himself back into the nearest chair and sighed heavily.

Astrid and Khalil sat flanking him on either side. Khalil rummaged through the papers on the table as Astrid spoke. "I just finished the last phase of conversion on the northeast city plot. That makes five city plots in all that are up and running. Any more and we might risk serious exposure."

"Yes, you're right. We have so much already." Keto grasped Astrid's hand as he leaned closer to her. "This is all thanks to you, my dear." He winked at her and patted her hand before turning back to Khalil.

"Is this what you come out here for? To rummage through my things?"

"It looks like you've been keeping busy, uncle. When do you think you will start to finally relax and enjoy your old age?"

"Don't worry, my boy. You'll get your chance to lead soon enough."

Fatima glided up the wide stairs from below carrying a wide platter with four cups and saucers and a decanter. She set the tray down on the near side and passed the servings out around the table. The four all sat inhaling the light aroma from the steam that billowed from the tea.

Keto sipped slowly and continued. "If you want to know what I've been up to, I can show you." He put the tea down next to a stack of drawings and assorted electronic tablets. He picked up the nearest tablet that still hummed softly and glowed a faint blue color. He began tapping away with his thumbs and the far wall that had been dark, lit up in a flare of sepia color.

The image it produced was a map of the surrounding area. All of the farm plots were illustrated in green and stood out from the somber beige background of the sand. In the center was a skeletal schematic of Pirate Town and all of its adjoining chambers, connecting the underground city to networks of tunnels leading all over the sector. On the far right of the map was the long and narrow fertile valley that ran from south to north.

Keto tapped the tablet he held a few more times and three sites on the map forming a triangle throbbed their skeletal schematic in bright red. "These are the new monitoring stations we've installed. As you can see they're spread out for maximum coverage of the surrounding area." A few more taps and wide, translucent circles grew from each of the sites covering all of the intervening space.

"The sensor clusters scan the area for motion as well as signals from aircraft and communications relays. Hopefully, we will be able to detect any unwanted guests before they get close enough to do or see anything." Keto stood energetically with the twinkle returning to his eye and wrapped a jalabiya around his stout form. "Come on, I'll show you how they work."

The group rose and followed their venerable leader back out into the blistering sun. Keto began to walk towards the sensor tower before freezing in his tracks. Astrid and Khalil followed his eyeline to see a man out in the desert expanse to the south-east. The trio stared with baited breath as the man approached from out of the swirling sands. The man wore a heavy poncho with a hood pulled down tight around his head. This was not traditional garb of anyone around here, even the neighboring Bambara that lived to the east.

"Fatima, go back inside." Keto instructed curtly, to which she promptly complied.

The howling wind made Keto's next utterance barely audible. "So, after all these years, he finally found us." Keto turned to his two companions. "Be prepared. I have been expecting this for some time, though I can honestly say I do not know *what* to expect."

Keto strode forward deliberately to meet the stranger and Astrid and Khalil followed closely behind. Before the two met Astrid recognized the smooth hunter's gait, like that of a tiger stalking its prey, as that of Colonel Eli Mazar.

"Hello Thaggaren Keto." A deep, raspy voice came from under the hood.

"Hello Mazar," Keto responded nonchalantly. "I've been expecting you."

"Hello Doctor Nielsen," Mazar said shifting his attention to his former charge.

"Hello," Astrid squeaked.

"You and I need to talk," Mazar said throwing back his hood to show a weary and aged face.

"What are you going to do?"

"Relax. I did not come here to corrupt your way of life or expose you to harm. I only want some answers."

The other Tuareg Keto and Khalil exchanged looks of relief with one another at this. A moment passed as the levity of the situation was absorbed, before Astrid said, "Listen, I know you're still mad from how things ended between us and…"

"Calm down, Astrid. Let us settle this tension between us and part as friends. I know why you did what you did, though at the time I must admit I was completely perplexed by your justifications." Mazar squinted as the wind picked up and the sand blew across his exposed face. "Is there somewhere we can go out of this weather?"

"Come." Keto said and the group hurried back to the bunker of the monitoring station.

The group entered the low-lying bunker. Keto was the first through the door, and waved Fatima away as the others filed through. Keto sat and Astrid, Khalil and Mazar all remained standing in the entrance.

Mazar spoke first. "I've been looking for you ever since we parted on such awkward terms. Never before that day had I failed so miserably."

Astrid opened her mouth to reply but Mazar continued. "But after forty two years in Security Operations, I can finally understand why you left. You wanted to help people, not in a theoretical sense, but in a visceral and practical way."

"Exactly! I am doing real good here, helping people who were struggling to survive. Listen, I want to apologize for not confronting you with this at the time. I'm sorry."

"You shouldn't be, because I would never have let you go if I had known your intentions at the time. It's just part of the job." Mazar stared into the middle distance for a moment before continuing, "You did the right thing for you and that's good enough for me. Transgenix got a project manager that was more than capable and everything fell into place just fine without you so don't apologize."

Mazar turned to the sitting Keto and squatted in front of his chair. "There is a lot I have learned since that day about human nature and I respect you for all you did for those under your care. Know now, that I will not expose you or your tribe. Your secret is safe with me."

He stood again and shook Keto's hand solemnly. Khalil sidled up beside Astrid and wrapped his arm around her waist. As Mazar turned back around, he observed this interplay and said, "I wish you both all of the happiness in the world."

Astrid threw her arms around Mazar's neck and hugged him as he stood there rigidly, before he finally softened and hugged her back. She let him go with tears in her eyes and Mazar shook Khalil's hand firmly before turning back to the door.

"Tell me before you go," Keto said standing, "how did you find us?"

"Sorry," Mazar replied, with a sly grin painting one corner of his mouth. "Trade secret. You have a very a nice garden here." He winked at Astrid before turning back to the door and throwing the hood of his poncho back over his head and disappearing back into the whiteout of sand.

Pirate Town:
Home Of The Tuaregs

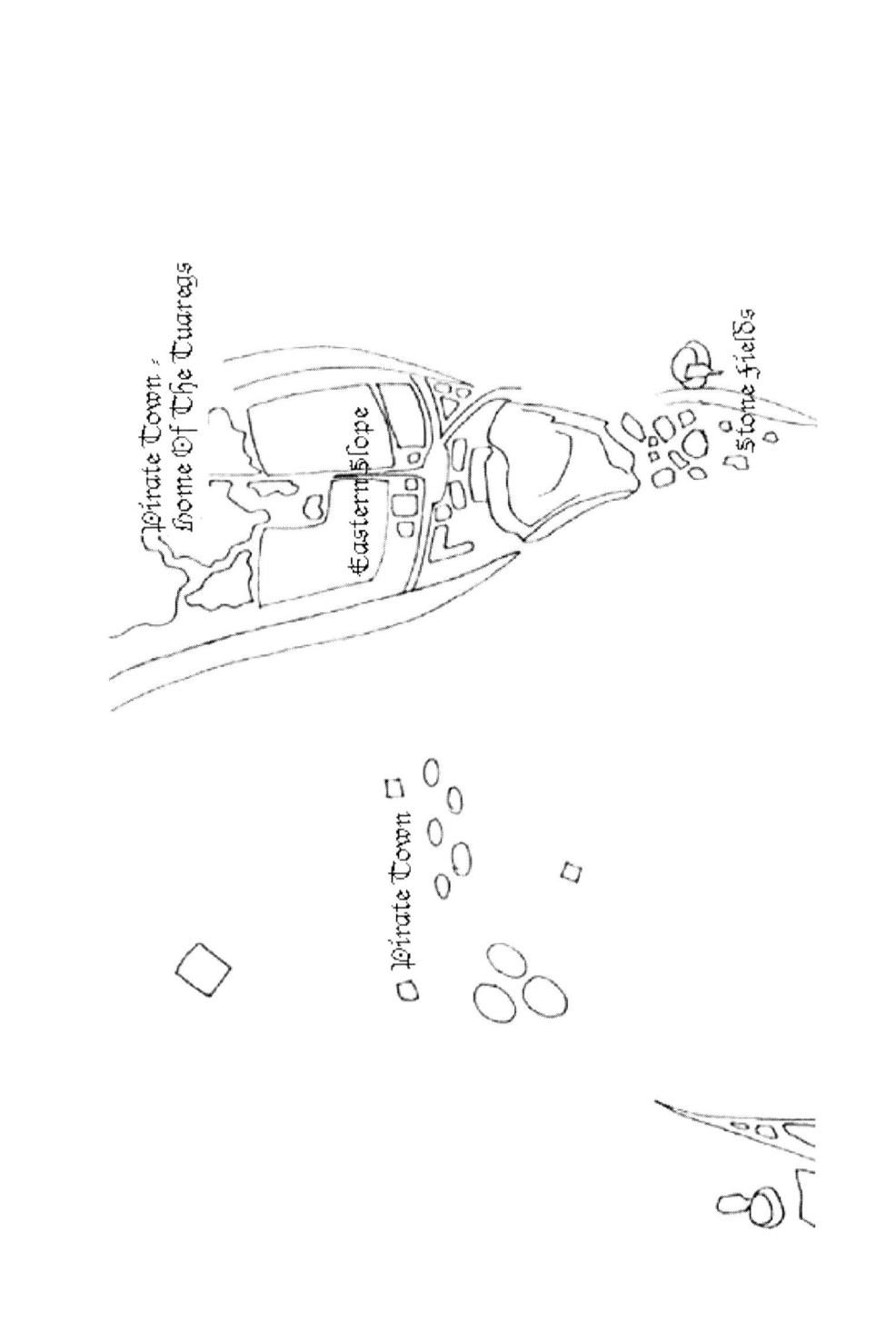

Eastern Slope

Stone fields

Pirate Town